Sherlock Holmes

And the

Irish Rebels

By

Kieran E· McMullen

Paperback ISBN 978-1-78092-053-5
ePub ISBN 978-1-78092-054-2
Mobipocket/Kindle ISBN 978-1-78092-055-9

Published in the UK by MX Publishing
335 Princess Park Manor, Royal Drive,
London, N11 3GX
www.mxpublishing.co.uk

Cover design by www.staunch.com

In memory

of

Vincent L. McMullen

Who gave me a love

Of God, Country,

Duty and Heritage

Special thanks to Dr. Dan Andriacco, Christina Johnson, Allyssa Roeske, Donna Cacy and especially Helen McMullen for all the help. I truly appreciate it!

CONTENTS

The Cast

Sherlock Holmes...AKA Liam Altamont

Dr John Watson.......................................AKA Dr Thomas Ryan

Colonel Flynn................Commander 3rd Australian Auxiliary Hospital

Mycroft Holmes...The British Civil Servant

Detective Sergeant Burns..............Dublin Metropolitan Police, G Division

Sean MacDiarmada.....................................Cofounder Irish Volunteers

Tom Clarke..........................Leader of the Irish Republican Brotherhood

Thomas MacDonagh.............................Irish Republican Brotherhood

Eamonn Ceannt....................................Irish Republican Brotherhood

Eoin MacNeill..Founder, Irish Volunteers

Bulmer Hobson.........Irish Volunteer, Cofounder Irish Scouting Movement

Michael Mallin................................Chief of Staff, Irish Citizen Army

James Connolly.....................................Founder, Irish Citizen Army

Padraig Pearse...President, Irish Republic

Sean Heuston..............................Volunteer, Commander at Mendicity

Joseph M. Plunkett................................Irish Republican Brotherhood

Edward (Ned) Daly.......................Volunteer, Commander at Four Courts

Willie Pearse....................................Irish Volunteer, brother of Padraig

Major John MacBride.................Commander, Irish Brigade in Boer War

Countess Constance Markievicz..... Second in Command St. Stephen's Green

Michael Collins..Aide de Camp to Plunkett

Captain Mahoney..................................Captured British Army Doctor

Lieutenant Chalmers..............................Captured British Army Officer

Winifred Carney.......................................Secretary to James Connolly

Michael O'Rahilly...Director of Arms, IV

Sir Matthew Nathan..................................Under Secretary for Ireland

Sir Augustine Birrell..................................Chief Secretary for Ireland

Major Ivor Price.......................................Military Intelligence Officer

Sean MacLoughlain..15 year old Volunteer

Father John O'Flanagan...Catholic Priest

General Sir John Maxwell...................Commander in Ireland after Rising

Mrs Martha Hudson...............................AKA Mrs Martha McGuffey

Constable Flood..Guard at Dublin Castle

Neville Chamberlain............................Chief, Royal Irish Constabulary

Robert Cacy...ICA Soldier

Michael Cusack...Informer for the IV

Sean Duffy..ICA Soldier

Jim Ryan...Medical Student

Forward

The episode which I relate in this book is the last adventure I had with my friend Sherlock Holmes, sponsored by his brother, Mycroft. While there was little mystery, there was much in the way of learning for me.

My stepmother had been Irish (as I related earlier in *Watson's Afghan Adventure*) and I had some sympathy for the land, though by no means was I truly cognizant of all its problems or its history. In fact, the schools of my day taught almost nothing about the island to our west. I knew more about America than I did about Ireland. This adventure changed my life and thinking probably more than my time in Afghanistan or my service in the Boer War.

Some will comment that I do not portray here the whole picture but merely segments of a bigger mural. That criticism is undoubtedly true for I was only involved in the smaller segments. Time and additional information give us the ability to see the broader view. We are later able to see all the actors on the stage. But when you're in the trench you can see only the mud and lumber walls, the slating under your feet and the barbed wire to your front. You are only worried about the man on your right, the one on your left and your enemy with his bayonet. All else - the politicians, the generals, the cannons to your rear, even though they impact your life - are out of your control and out of your thoughts.

So here I recorded what I saw and what I did during the war within a war. I came to it with few preconceptions and left it with grave misgivings.

Holmes had changed his role in life. He was no longer "the great detective" but now, since the adventure I recorded as "His Last Bow" he had continued to be "the great spy". It was a role he did not treasure. He performed it out of duty and he did it well, as he did all things.

As I write this, the Great War has ended and the victor nations are gathering in Paris. I understand that the Irish have sent a delegation to try and get recognition for an independent country. I'm sure no one will listen, not even the American President Wilson. I fear we are not done in Ireland.

John Watson, MD

Lieutenant Colonel, RAMC

Sherlock Holmes
And the
Irish Rebels

Chapter 1

Wednesday

12 April 1916

It had been a good year and a half since I had last seen Holmes. In fact, it had been since the day after we had captured the German spy, Von Bork, on the English coast in 1914. Von Bork had thought he was buying British naval codebooks from an Irish-American named Altamont. In fact, Von Bork bought a trip to his homeland and we had rounded up his entire spy organization. Not only had Holmes fooled Von Bork, he had even inserted Mrs Hudson in Von Bork's home as his housekeeper. It was a wonderful piece of work for the Home Office. I eventually related this case in a piece I called "His Last Bow". I was wrong to have done so!

Having heard nothing from my friend in over a year it was with some amazement that I opened a telegram from him on the 12th of April 1916: "Lieutenant Colonel John Watson, MD., 3rd Australian Auxiliary Hospital, Dartford, Kent. Come Dublin immediately stop. See Mycroft at Diogenes on way stop. Altamont."

I was puzzled, to say the least. Why was Holmes still using the name Altamont (he used Liam for a Christian name) and why was he in Dublin? Was he still working for the Home Office?

My own story since last seeing Holmes was quite

simple. With the coming of the Great War, I had offered my services to the Army Medical Department. At first, I had been thanked but turned down. Surely, the war wouldn't last beyond Christmas. After all, it was England, France and Russia against Germany and Austria-Hungry. We had our foe caught on two fronts, and one might call our Italian ally the third front. We had very effectively divided his strength. His supply lines from overseas were cut off by our overwhelming naval power.

But as the months progressed and the war took on a world-wide aspect, the Medical Department found they had a use for me, a 64-year-old-former-campaigner. I had not seen service since my volunteer days in the Boer War. Back then, the Army had been stretched thin also, between the Boxers in China, disruptions in the Sudan and the Boers in South Africa, men were needed.

Now, however, in my more senior years, even the "New Army" felt I was of some use in the rearward hospitals. I had been assigned as Liaison Officer from the British Army Medical Department to an Australian hospital that specialized in the care of shell shocked soldiers. It was a large facility in Kent that took care of 1400 men. These men had seen the worst that the trenches had to offer. My primary job was to make sure that the British Army Medical Department provided all support possible to our Commonwealth soldiers. To do this, essentially supply function, I had a staff of three exemplary non-commissioned officers, which gave me time to help with the overwhelming patient workload.

In later years, shell-shock would be a disparaging term

so we would classify officers as having "neurasthenia" and enlisted men as having "hysteria". But for now, they were either "shell-shock: wounded" or "shell-shock: sick". Shell-shock: wounded was largely applied to those who had actually seen battle in the trenches. This was considered an honourable thing. Shell-shock: sick, for the most part, had seen no actual combat.

During their stay at our hospital, these men were treated with all the latest methods and all the finest care. They were given all the current treatments from sedatives to electric shock therapy. In many cases, merely a calming atmosphere was all that was needed, along with an understanding that fear was a natural thing. Fear, many times, is what keeps us alive and responding, but fear must be controlled and thought of as a useful tool.

Soldiers who stayed here were issued "Hospital Blues". It consisted of a medium blue suit and red ties. It seemed to give our patients a sense of unity and belonging. It also made them easy to identify if they decided on a private "vacation" from the grounds.

Those who recovered were sent to a Command Depot for re-assignment to an active unit. Those who did not recover but were capable of functioning in a society without cannons were given a silver war badge and discharged from service with the thanks of His Majesty's Government.

There were some who would never recover.

It was while I was pondering the telegram from Holmes that a corporal came to fetch me from my office.

3

"Commander needs to see you, sir. Said it was important."

I looked up, startled out of my thoughts. "Yes, of course. Tell Colonel Flynn I'll be right there."

The orderly was off almost before I finished speaking. I took a quick look at the mirror on my north wall before heading down the corridor to the Commanding Office.

"Nice old goat in the mirror," I thought. "Still has a full head of reddish-brown hair, a grey moustache I admit, but still spry and presentable. Tie straight." I looked down, "boots could use a brush. Ah, well, this is war. I wonder what Holmes wanted me for."

I hustled down the corridor to the Colonel's office on the west side. Entering his outer office, the orderly who had been sent for me came to attention behind his desk.

"Right in, sir. Colonel said don't wait."

"Thank you, Burton," I responded, passing him and opening the door to Flynn's office.

"John, come in mate," came the booming voice of our Commander. "Sit down; you know I hate this military formality stuff. Be glad when all this is over and I can go back to private practice.

"Well," he grinned, glancing at his papers as I took a seat next to his desk. "Looks like we're losing you. Know what's going on?"

"I'm sure you know more than I do, Colonel. I was just

going to come and talk to you when I got your message. I've received a request from an old friend to come to Dublin post haste, though I don't know why."

"Looks like it's you who knows more, John. All I got was a telegram from the Home Office and another from the Medical Department Headquarters, almost at the same time. Here."

Flynn handed me two telegram sheets. The first, from the Medical Department, simply stated I was to be seconded to the Home Office, effective immediately. I was not to await my replacement but to report at once.

The second telegram, this from the Home Office, assigned me to Special Branch, Scotland Yard. "Report immediately to Mr Mycroft Holmes at his usual location."

"What the devil do they want me for?"

"I'd hoped you'd tell me, John." Flynn leaned back in his chair and looked at the ceiling as if trying to think of something. "Special Branch. Is that the outfit they used to call Special Irish Branch?"

"I believe so. Why?"

"Oh, nothing. They're who I have to thank for my mum ending up in Australia is all." He laughed and stood up from the desk. "Well you, my friend, had best make arrangements. Can you leave tonight?"

"No. I've got patients I must transition to someone tonight and I won't go off without doing that, even for Holmes.

5

I've also got to pack a kit and arrange to store the rest. I'll take the first train in the morning. Mycroft can wait 14 hours for me to get there.

Flynn laughed again and coming forward, patted me on the back. "I'll be very sorry to lose you, John, you have been a tremendous help here. I only hope your replacement is half as good."

"Kind words, sir. I hope I'm not gone too long. I'm sure whoever they send to replace me will do just as well. In the meantime, Sergeant Locke will make sure your support line stays intact."

With that, we shook hands and I departed to make arrangements for the care of my patients.

Later that night I was packing the majority of my books and belongings into boxes that Sergeant Locke had procured for me. Not knowing what the mission was that required the assistance of an old fellow was driving me to distraction.

Why was Holmes still calling himself Altamont? Were there German spies in Ireland? Coast watchers perhaps, reporting our ship movements to Germany by wireless?

Then the thought suddenly came to me. Yes. It must be a German plot. After all, hadn't Martha Hudson moved to Dublin last year? And when I wrote to her, on receiving the assignment in Kent, she had written back that she had opened a rooming house on Talbot Street and taken to using her maiden name of McGuffey!

How stupid of me! I thought it odd at the time, but I had no idea Holmes was in Ireland. He had never returned the letters I had written to him in Sussex. And I had to admit that though I was too busy to look carefully, I had seen nothing in the newspaper about Holmes and any investigations or war work.

I spent the rest of the night visiting with two of my colleagues, discussing my current cases and the status of each soldier. I was concerned that in one or two cases the simple change of doctors would set the poor fellows back a bit. Having transferred cases, packed a traveling kit and boxed my belongings, I thanked Locke for his help and tried to get a few hours sleep. Unknown to me at the time, I was about to enter one of the most bewildering chapters of my life. For now, I would get a bit of sleep before catching the early train to London.

Chapter 2

Thursday

13 April 1916

Finding that sleep was useless, I was up especially early to make the train out of Dartford to London. With uniform on and bag in hand, I appeared on the train platform a half hour early. Taking a seat on one of the many empty benches, my mind continued to churn. Holmes, I thought, would not have this problem. He would merely say "One cannot make bricks without clay" and turn his mind to other things. I had never been able to achieve this.

Finally, the train came. Taking a seat in a smoking compartment, I drew out my pipe to pass an hour. Instead, it was almost two hours before we arrived at Victoria. However, much to my surprise, as I left the platform, I was met by a young Private (they all seemed so young) who saluted and asked if I were Lieutenant Colonel Watson. When I replied that I was, he informed me that he had been sent with a motor car to take me to my meeting with a Mr Holmes at the Diogenes Club[1].

It was nice to be back in London. As we drove through the streets I couldn't help but be amazed at the huge number of

---

[1] A club for "unclubable men" of which Mycroft was a founder.

uniformed men and even woman. British, Australian, New Zealanders, Indian, French, Italian; soldiers, nurses, auxiliaries - it was astounding. As the streets bustled it seemed business as usual. Hard to believe that these same people were terrorized at night by the comings and goings of German LZ-90's[2] dropping their cargo of deadly bombs.

Our few minutes journey over, I walked up the familiar steps of the Diogenes Club and was ushered into the foyer before I had a chance to ring the bell. Having been reminded of the rules of silence[3], except in the stranger's room, and my hat taken, I was led by the major-domo to the Stranger's Room where Holmes and I had met with Mycroft on at least four occasions.

As the door opened, I saw nothing that reminded me of the old days. Instead, there was a bustling operation centre. Half a dozen uniformed men were busy with tasks I knew would be critical to the war effort. The large windows had been covered with heavy curtains and on the far wall were two telephone switchboards, telegraph keys and tickertapes. Desks rowed both sides and on the wall opposite the window were bulletin boards filled with papers. In the middle of the room was a gigantic map board of Europe, Asia and Africa. The board was covered with coloured pins and two sergeants were busy reading telegraphs and changing pin locations. Mycroft, one hand on his hip, the other stroking his chin, was looking intently at the map.

"Sergeant, see if we can't get better information on the

---

[2] Baron Von Zeppelin's rigid air ships.
[3] No member was allowed to speak to another in the club.

strength of Von Lettow. We're wasting far too many resources in Africa," said Mycroft.

"Yes, sir. I'll get the wire off immediately," replied the Sergeant.

Mycroft looked up and realizing I was present, came forward with hand outstretched.

"My dear doctor, how good of you to come so quickly. You're looking quite well. Being in harness is doing you good! Excellent. Excellent!" Shaking my hand vigorously, he continued, "But come, come. I have a little office to myself over here, used to be a coat closet, but it does for my needs. Come in and have a seat."

We crossed the buzzing room and entered a small cubby hole just big enough for a table to be used as a desk and three straight backed chairs. As we passed into the room, Mycroft rang for the major-domo and asked me to have a seat.

"Somewhere under all those papers there is a chair, Watson. Just pile it on the floor. Good Lad. Ah, Hancock, I know it's not quite noon, but bring the Colonel and me a brandy, will you? Sit, Watson, please. Let me just close the door. Hancock will knock when he has our drinks."

"Do your members approve of what you've done to the Stranger's Room?" I asked, smiling.

"Ah, well, all for the war effort. I needed somewhere to work where I wouldn't be disturbed constantly, and this is, shall we say, out of sight, out of mind."

Hancock knocked on the door and entered. After placing the brandies on the table he asked if there was anything else.

"No, Hancock. We'll have lunch in an hour, but nothing until then.

With that, Hancock departed. "To your health, Doctor," said Mycroft, lifting his glass. "And yours" I replied, doing the same.

Mycroft hadn't changed significantly in the years since I had seen him. A little heavy for his height, hair now white, and the hairline seemed to have receded significantly, but at 69, he seemed as quick and sharp as ever.

"Well, Watson," he finally said, putting down his glass. "Yes, I know I'm still overweight and have lost quite a bit of my hair, but you're right, I haven't lost a step when it comes to my job."

"But, I…"

"From your face and eyes. You must be a terrible card player."

"Yes," I smiled, "I'm much better at billiards."

"Well, down to business. Do you know why you're here?"

"Only that Sherlock is evidently still playing the role of Liam Altamont, that he is in Dublin, that Mrs Hudson, or should I say, McGuffey, is there also and that he has sent for me. Other than that, I know nothing."

"Excellent, Watson. Yes indeed. We have convinced Sherlock to stay on the job and Mrs Hudson has agreed to play a part as she did with the Von Burk affair."

"But how can Sherlock use a persona which the Germans must know is false if he's looking for German spies? Surely, Von Bork blew the whistle on him as soon as he got back to Germany."

Mycroft looked down at his brandy and swirled it in the glass. "Perhaps Watson, Von Bork never got back to Germany. Perhaps he has been held incommunicado for the last eighteen months just so Sherlock could continue to use his disguise as an English hating, pro-German, Irish-American."

I squirmed in my seat. "Is that legal? He was a diplomat."

"Let us say, necessary, shall we?"

"All right. I can accept that. But are there so many spies in Ireland?"

"Worse than that, I'm afraid," he said with a smirk. "There are so many Irish."

I sat looking at him for a moment, not knowing exactly how to take the remark. My confusion showed.

"How much do you know about the current situation in Ireland?"

"Not a lot, I'm afraid. I know we're not conscripting in Ireland and the number of recruits has fallen terribly since the war started. Also, that Home Rule has been delayed until after the war. More than that, I'm afraid I've been too busy to notice."

"Unfortunately," said Mycroft, "Your understanding is all too common in Great Britain. Segments of Ireland are a boiling cauldron, both for the Union and for complete independence." He stood up and paced back and forth in the small space behind his desk.

"The problem," he said, turning to look at me "is the damned Irish won't be English and we can't be fighting there as well as everywhere else."

"Mycroft, you have surely lost me. Are you saying there is going to be rebellion? Why? Why now?"

"Because 'England's difficulty is Ireland's opportunity', as the saying goes. How many rebellions have we had there since Henry II made the mistake of invading? Just in the last 120 years there have been risings in 1798, 1803, 1848 and 1867. And believe me, unless we act, there will be another one soon."

"I'm afraid, sir, you'll have to explain it to me," I said. "I thought all was quiet, for now anyway."

"Let me give you the short version. In my opinion, since the incorporation of Ireland into the United Kingdom in 1801, we have made a great error. Ireland has been treated like a colony instead of an equal with this island. They've been in the parliament, yes. But we pass special laws which treat Ireland separately. Remember, they had their own Parliament until the Union. In recent years, there has been a huge revival of Irish games and music and the Irish language. And where Dublin was once the second city of the empire, it is now filled with decaying tenements. Tenements are rich turf for rebels. The industry has moved to the Northeast of Ireland which is heavily Protestant and heavily pro-union. The South is Catholic, nationalist and poor. Now that's a generality, but largely true. It's also true that most Irish want Home Rule, but those that don't are vehement in staying with the Union. The majority want a peaceful existence with dominion status like Canada."

"Why don't they just take an island-wide vote to see what the people want to do?" I asked.

"No, too many people have too much involved. It would surely go for Home Rule and the Ulster Unionists will take up arms to prevent that."

"What? Rebel to stay not rebel to go? I'm confused."

"Watson, in 1912, Sir Edward Carson formed the Ulster Volunteer Force, or UVF. They dedicated themselves to keeping Ireland in the Union even if it meant by force. They knew the majority of Ireland wanted Home Rule but were afraid of a Nationalist Catholic majority in Dublin. They claimed 'Home Rule means Rome Rule.' Not true of course, but to them, a real fear none the less.

"In April of '14, while you and Holmes were busy tracking Von Bork, Carson armed the UVF in violation of import and licensing laws. He imported 25,000 magazine rifles and 3 million rounds of ammunition and distributed them to a now well organized para-military organization."

Putting my glass back on the table, I turned back in my

14

chair thinking. "And we did nothing?"

"Yes, Watson. Plans were started to take the weapons back but that would mean bloodshed and the army. And the army in Ireland was officered by Unionists who let it be known that they would not lead their soldiers in the task of disarming the UVF. The officers at Curragh, almost to a man, would resign their commissions rather than lead their soldiers against fellow Unionists."

"And the government permitted this type of behaviour?"

"Yes, in fact, large segments of the Parliament found it quite satisfying."

"But the Arms Act," I protested.

"The Arms Act has not been in effect in Ireland since 1906, old fellow. Another one of those ways we seem to have one set of rules for us and another set for Ireland. Since '06 it has been easier to buy and sell guns there than in England. Still, one needed an import license and a local license, but those were easy to get and you didn't need two magistrates to sign the license. But the fact is the law wasn't really enforced anyway. The outcome was this: you remember the labour riots in the larger cities in '13?"

I nodded.

"Yes, well," he continued, "the police badly over-reacted. People killed and injured, didn't look good to the working classes. Anyway, two men, Larkin and Connolly had been union organizers. When the disturbances happened, they formed a group called the Irish Citizen Army or ICA to protect the strikers from the police. For the most part they were unarmed but again in a Para-military format. Also, a man named MacNeill formed the Irish National Volunteers, still another group to contend with! Both the ICA and the Volunteers were for Irish independence. Peacefully, if possible, but violently if need be."

"But Home Rule is on the books," I said. "It's only held off until after the war."

"Home Rule, Watson, will not happen! Carson and the unionists won't stand for it. One way or the other, there will be bloodshed.

"But let me continue. Since the UVF imported weapons without consequence, the Volunteers decided they must arm also, and so they did. Not as well, I admit. They brought in 1500 single shot German Mausers to Howth and Kilcoole and I believe 25,000 rounds of ammunition. Now both sides were armed. But in the case of the Nationalists, there was an attempt by civil authority, using the Army, to take the weapons. They didn't get but eight or ten but the real tragedy was that the army opened fire on unarmed civilians at Bachelor's Walk on the River Liffey. Civilians were killed and the Nationalists could tell the people, 'see how England treats you!' Oh, the Army was provoked by the crowd. But their response played into the hands of the Nationalists."

"But where is the government in all this?" I replied.

"Nowhere!"

"What?"

"Both sides drill openly with weapons and posture about and the Irish government takes the attitude that it is better to do nothing."

"I can't believe all this."

"It's too true, I assure you, Watson. Once the war started, they believed things would calm down and the Irish would come to the defence of the Empire. At first it did. Carson's UVF enlisted en-masse. John Redmond, the leader of the Irish Parliamentary Party and who had orchestrated the Home Rule Bill had largely wrested the Irish National Volunteers from the more radical elements and offered the Volunteers for service with the army. He also agreed to hold Home Rule in abeyance. The decision to wait on Home Rule split the Volunteers. A good 80 percent went with Redmond. The rest went with MacNeill and became the Irish Volunteers, or IV, about 11,000 men."

"And it's the Volunteers who are causing trouble?" I asked.

"No end, I'm afraid. Marching about, telling young men not to enlist, seditious speeches and being generally a nuisance. Them and the ICA."

"And the Lord Lieutenant and other officials, what of them?"

"The current Lord Lieutenant is a fool named Ivor Churchill, Lord Wimbourne. Of course, his position is mostly

17

ceremonial. No real power. The Chief Secretary, who should really be running things, is Augustine Birrell, but since he is also a member of the cabinet and we've been at war, he spends most of his time in London. His sympathies are plainly with the Nationalists.

"The Undersecretary, Sir Matthew Nathan, is competent enough, but left on his own he is a 'business-as-usual' type who does not have the insightfulness to deal with the Irish. He too, I fear sympathizes with the Nationalists."

Mycroft sat back down at the table. "That, I believe is the big picture. Another brandy?" He lifted the decanter and I held out my glass without even thinking about it.

"Well," I said, sitting back again in my chair, "I would think that Redmond used exactly the wrong tactic."

"What would you have done?"

"Well, wouldn't he have been better off to withhold all the Volunteers until Home Rule had been implemented and provided them as a dominion force rather than playing the co-operative parliamentarian?"

"It's what I would have done in his place surely. Wait for the UVF to march off to war, decreasing Ulster's ability to resist Home Rule and put down whatever little trouble there was with Irish troops."

"Who supplied all the weapons?"

"Industrialists to the UVF. Irish-Americans supplied the money to the Volunteers. The Germans were happy to supply them to the Nationalists. Through the Dutch, of course."

"And the Volunteers, they're the same as the Sein Feiners?"

"No, Sein Fein is a political party which professes non-violent solutions, but since all Nationalists are lumped together by the government, the terms Volunteers and Sein Feiners are used interchangeably. The SF does hate everything English."

"Well, it's all very confusing, but what am I doing here?" I asked, leaning forward and putting down my glass.

"Doctor, Sherlock has need of a companion he can rely on with absolute certainty and he has asked for you. He has continued with his disguise of this person, Altamont, an Irish-American, English hater and has made himself a part of the Volunteers. He has worked himself up in their circles but has failed to get the information he needs.

"There is one more level to this puzzle, Watson. It's called the IRB, the Irish Republican Brotherhood. There are some who believe they are the ones actually in charge of what is going on. Sherlock and I know they are. Their leader is a man named Thomas Clarke. He has quite a history; bomber, prisoner, naturalized American and willing to do anything for the "Cause". It's this inner secret society that Sherlock has tried to infiltrate.

"There is going to be a rebellion in Ireland, and soon! On St. Patrick's Day last, the entire volunteer organization held a parade, a huge affair, in which they passed in review of their leader, MacNeill. We believe it was a dress rehearsal for a rising."

"And the RIC didn't stop it?"

"The Royal Irish Constabulary has no authority in Dublin. The Dublin Metropolitan Police do and the DMP is an unarmed force. But I'll let Sherlock explain all this to you tomorrow. What you need to know is this. Three days ago, a shipment of arms left Germany for Ireland. So did Sir Roger Casement."

"Sir Roger?" I was startled. "But he's a friend of Doyle's. What was he doing in Germany?"

"Your editor's friend did great service in Peru and in Belgian Congo, for which he was knighted. But he is also an Irish Nationalist and he has been spending the last few months trying to raise an "Irish Brigade" from among the POW's in German camps, to come home and fight for Ireland instead of England. He has been singularly unsuccessful."

"I would think so. Soldiers who have fought together, stay together. They don't go off with the enemy."

"Yes, well, not even Birrell knows of the arms shipment or Casement's movements. He'll be told when he needs to know. We can't let the Germans know we can read their codes, and that means not telling anyone who doesn't have to know. You, Doctor, are going to have to travel to Dublin on tomorrow's boat train. You will carry nothing that might be used to identify you as John Watson."

"Alright, but I'll need….."

Mycroft held up his hand. "Already done. From here you will go to your hotel, your room is here." He handed me a key. "In the room you will find clothes. They're not new, but they are all American manufacture and should fit you well. In the jacket will be dollars, a few pounds and an American passport. Sewn into your waistcoat, behind the breast pocket, will be a letter from the Home Secretary giving your true identity. Do not lose it."

"And may I ask who and what I am to portray?"

"You are Dr Thomas Elmer Ryan of San Francisco and a member of the Irish-American Clan na Gael and a friend of John Devoy, the clan's head."

"But I know Ryan. The last time I saw him was in San Francisco 25 years ago."

"We know," he smiled. "The two years you spent in San Francisco means you know the city. If questioned, you don't have to memorize or lie, you can answer from experience."

"But where is Ryan?"

"Dead. Died on a trip to Argentina a few months ago. He hadn't been active in the Clan in years and Devoy is probably unaware of his death. Since Ryan was educated in Scotland and lived in America, you'd best use your best American idioms." Mycroft smiled. "Leave your kit in your room, we'll collect it. You'll find everything you need there, all American. Even a Colt automatic pistol and some ammunition."

"Anything else?"

21

"Altamont will meet you at the dock, Dr Ryan," said Mycroft, extending his flipper of a hand and rising. "Best of luck to you."

I rose and we shook hands. As I retraced my steps through the now busy strangers room, I paused to look at the map. In Ireland were four red pins for troops in country: Curragh, Dublin, Belfast and Athlone. Maybe four thousand soldiers in all. *There best not be a rising*, I thought as I left the Diogenes Club.

On leaving the Diogenes Club, I found the same soldier who had picked me up at the Victoria waiting for me. But now he was dressed as a taxi driver and holding open the door to his vehicle.

"A man of many talents, I see," I quipped.

He smiled and saluted. "I'll be picking you up in the morning, sir, at seven to take you to the boat train. Here's your ticket." He handed me an envelope. "I'm afraid I'm taking you to a second class hotel, but it's the one we use for these sorts of things."

"Don't worry about me, son. I'm happy with just a blanket."

Within fifteen minutes we were at the hotel. It was not all bad, catering to the traveling businessman. Entering the room, I found a well-used traveling bag on the bed. In it was the usual underclothing and toiletries one would expect. There was also a note.

"Push down on bottom of bag. Spring latch."

I turned the bag on its top and pushing down on the corners of the bag, heard a faint click. The bag's bottom came off and in a narrow space I found the promised pistol and three magazines of ammunition. There was also an American passport in my assumed name, along with hotel bills, a Cunard ticket from the week before and a letter addressed to me at the hotel, all in my new name. Mycroft surely thought of everything. I removed the papers but returned the pistol to its hiding place. It was a .32 Colt pocket pistol, light and easy to carry. On the bed was a good set of American-made clothes. Not new, obviously worn, but not shabby. The labels were from a haberdasher on Mott Street in San Francisco. I tried on my new clothes - they fit very well - and packed up my uniform, placing everything in a large box I found in the corner of the room. It was already labelled with my name. You couldn't doubt Mycroft's efficiency.

I contented myself that night with reading all the newspapers I could find, looking for any clues to the problems in Ireland. Most of the news, of course, was about the war. It seemed that no one was paying any attention to the Irish question.

Chapter 3

Friday

14 April 1916

True to his word, my young soldier showed up with his taxi at exactly seven in the morning. "Euston Station, sir?" he said in a loud voice.

"Exactly, buddy." I said in my best pseudo-American. The driver laughed and shook his head as he opened the door. Inside, I found Mycroft.

"I didn't expect to see you again, sir." I said, sitting next to him.

"Just need to pass on a little bit of information," he said as the motor car started from the curb. "Our latest intelligence tells us that the rising is to be on Holy Saturday, the twenty second. Now, they already have a three-day exercise planned starting on Easter, so it wouldn't take much to move up the timetable a day. Let Sherlock know, though he probably already does."

"Certainly. Any news on the arms?"

"No, all we know for sure is that the ship has left port. The navy is searching for it, and they'll find it," he said confidently.

As we drove up to Euston Station, Mycroft touched me on the arm. "This is a more serious situation than anyone in the government wants to admit. Be careful, Doctor. We're not as young as we once were."

I smiled back as I exited the taxi. I was touched by Mycroft's concern. "And not as old as you might think," I smiled. Taking my bag from the driver I walked to the platform.

To tell the truth, I actually got more sleep on the train than I had the night before in the hotel. While the bed was comfortable enough, my mind raced all night thinking of what-ifs. Now with the rocking of the train, I fell into a deep sleep and it was only the calling of the conductor that woke me at Holyhead.

I transferred to the RMS Leinster, the Dublin Holyhead mail boat. (The reader may remember this vessel was some two years later torpedoed in the Irish Sea with the loss of over 500, almost all soldiers.)

The trip to Dublin Port was quite a miserable affair. The seas were rough this time of year and everyone watched the ocean's surface for any sign of U-boats. The chances were, of course, very slim indeed. None the less, there was always a nagging suspicion.

It was only an hour before sunset when the ferry finally docked at Dublin Port and true to form, there was Holmes, cloth cap, celluloid collar and of all things, a moustache. Raising his hand from across the street he shouted, "Hey Doc, how are ya?" He was indeed, still affecting his American persona.

We clasped hands and Holmes relieved me of my bag, slapping me on the back. "Great to see you again. Come on with

25

me." Stepping back to the kerb he hailed a cab. "Talbot Street," he told the cabby and settled back on the seat. "We'll talk when we get to the roomin' house, Doc, okay?"

"Certainly," I said, and had a hard time not laughing at my friend.

As we passed through the city, Holmes pointed out places of interest. From Sackville Street we turned right at Nelson's Pillar onto Earl Street and in a minute, we were at "Mrs McGuffey's" rooming house, which was a walk-up over a grocers.

Coming up the steps we were greeted by Martha Hudson. "Oh, Doctor!" she cried, "It's been so long. How are you? I'll have tea in a moment. You have the room next to Mr Altamont and the next I've kept empty for you and him to use as your sitting room." With that she gave me a hug and as she scurried away I could hear her chuckling, "Altamont, what a name, couldn't you use O'Brien or something?"

"Well, come in, Doctor, come in," said Holmes, passing on along the hall to the sitting room. Throwing my bag under the table, I looked about at the comfortable, if under-furnished, room with its south window, bookcase, sideboard, table and four chairs.

"Not the lap of luxury, but it will do." I said.

"Sit down, Doc."

I looked askance at Holmes. "Really, do you have to?"

"Ryan, it's best to be in character at all times. That way

at a critical moment you are less likely to give yourself away."

"All right, buddy," I said, turning a chair around and straddling it. I folded my arms over the chair back and grinned. Holmes could not help but laugh.

"All right, Doctor. You win. In here, we are ourselves."

"Fine. Fine. Ah, Mrs McGuffey, the tea, how nice of you." Mrs Hudson deposited pot and cups and biscuits on the table.

"I do hope, Doctor, that you'll hurry Mr Altamont along now that you're here so we can all go home."

"Don't you like it here?" I asked.

"Oh, it's nice enough, sir, but it isn't home, is it?"

"I understand Mrs McGuffey. I surely do."

Once Mrs McGuffey (for so I shall call her from now on) had left and Holmes had poured our tea I could hold my tongue no longer.

"Tell me, Holmes. What are we supposed to be doing?"

"How much did Mycroft tell you," he asked.

"Not enough about what you're doing. He said you'd fill me in. His was basically a broad brush. He did tell me to tell you that they believe there is to be a rising on Holy Saturday."

"Hmmm, possible but I doubt it. Much more likely for Easter itself. What else?"

27

"Well, the Germans are sending a boatload of weapons, and Sir Roger Casement is supposedly on his way here from Germany. I can't believe he was trying to recruit our soldiers for rebellion."

"Yes, I know he convinced your friend Doyle to be for Home Rule but it's a big jump to treason." He pulled out his briar pipe and started packing it from a pouch. "The German ship is supposed to have 25,000 captured Russian rifles, ten machine guns and a million rounds of ammunition."

"My God, what horror that could do!"

"True, Watson. But I'm sure our Navy is up to the task of finding it." He took a long puff, "And sending it to the bottom."

We sat quietly for a moment. Finally I took out my pipe (the one thing I kept from my kit) and started to fill it, waiting for Holmes to continue.

"Casement's efforts were fairly futile. He only got about fifty men to volunteer and most of them aren't worth a tinker's damn. One IRB man, named Montieth, made his way to Germany, through America, to help him recruit. Seems to be the only competent help he has."

"Oh, IRB?" I asked.

"Yes, Irish Republican Brotherhood. It really is a secret society. They are the ones planning the rebellion."

"Holmes, I really wish you'd explain things. I thought the Volunteers were planning the rising."

Holmes grinned and took another puff. "Watson, nothing in Ireland is simple but let me see if I can explain our position.

"First, my name of course, is Liam Altamont. I'm an American and employed in Dublin Castle as a telegrapher. That gives me easy access to Major Price, the intelligence chief and my prime contact. My other contact is Detective Sergeant Burns of the Dublin Metropolitan Police, but we'll get back to them.

"Because I'm an Irish-American with a Nationalist bend and a job that gets me in and out of Dublin Castle, I've been approached by members of the Irish Volunteers to supply them with information. This I have done over the past year. I even helped them unload rifles at Howth and hid them around Dublin."

"No, surely not."

"Oh, it wouldn't matter one way or the other, they were going to import arms and Birrell wouldn't make waves about it. After all, the Unionists had them. Anyway, I'm well trusted in the Volunteers though I hold no actual post. By the way, you, Doctor, have been employed by the military hospital which is now in the Castle. Major Price has arranged everything. He is the only one besides myself who knows who you are. I will, of course, introduce you around as my friend from the States and as a friend of Devoy's, our benefactor in the US. You haven't seen him in years. "

Holmes poured out the last of the tea before continuing.

"To finish out about your contacts, if you need to get a message to Price or to Burns but can't get to the Castle, give it to Mrs McGuffey. She'll take it to a fishmonger down on the quays from where it will make its way.

"Price is a good, honest fellow. You'll meet him tomorrow. As to Burns, I'll say nothing. I would like your impression when you meet him. He is a member of the G-division. There are only about sixteen members of that force. Besides investigating major crimes they are the ones who keep an eye on the Nationalists. Most work out of Great Brunswick Street but Burns has an office at the College Street Station."

"You mentioned a secret group called the IRB, Holmes. Just who are they?"

"Now you get down to the crux of the matter, Watson. For it's the IRB that's planning the rising. Had I come here as a returning Irishman, I might have been accepted into the Brotherhood, but as it is, as an American, I'm trusted only to a point.

"Within the ranks of the Irish Volunteers are members of the Brotherhood. The IRB is for violent overthrow of the government, where even now, most of the Volunteers see hope for a peaceful solution to Irish Independence. Even the leader of the Volunteers, MacNeill, doesn't know that senior members of the IRB are using his organization to ferment rebellion behind his back.

"I also know that James Connolly, while not IRB, is in on the plot. I'll take you to Liberty Hall later tonight and introduce you to the 'players' in our little act. It's quite a varied assortment."

"Why doesn't DMP just shut all this down?"

"Because DMP can't get close enough to what's going on. Every DMP man is known as well as their informants. Not that the DMP doesn't also know all the Volunteers, of course they do, but each side knows not to talk."

Holmes looked out the window into the early darkness. "What say we go ahead and go to Liberty Hall now, Watson? No time like the present and it's only a few blocks."

As we rose to leave, Mrs McGuffey came in to get the tea service. "Need a late supper, Mr Altamont?"

"No, Mrs McGuffey. The doctor and I are going for a walk and we'll find something to eat while we're out."

"Very good, sir," she replied. "And Doctor," she added, stopping at the door, "like old times, it is."

Putting on my new felt hat, I started walking with Holmes back toward the quays. I looked about at everything, trying to orient myself to the new city. Holmes looked over at me.

"It is fairly easy to get around in Dublin, Doctor. Just don't go into that rabbit warren north of the Four Courts[4]. Dangerous and easy to get lost in the alleys."

"I'll remember that," I said. As we came into Beresford Place, I stood back and looked at the building called Liberty Hall, the headquarters of the Irish Citizen Army and the labour union they were formed to protect. Across the front of the

---

[4] Area of slums north of the Administrative and Judicial Courts Buildings.

building was a large banner "We serve neither King nor Kaiser, but Ireland"

I turned to Holmes. "Well you can't say you don't know where they stand, can you?"

"No," he replied. "Hopefully, some of the people I want you to meet will be here. The Volunteer Headquarters is across the river on Dawson Street. But the real leaders, the IRB members meet here with Connolly, or at the tobacco shop of Thomas Clarke over on Great Britain Street. Clarke is the real power behind this whole affair, and the money comes from John Devoy, the American Clan Na Gael leader. Neither Devoy nor Clarke know we read all their messages to their German allies."

"How?"

"Devoy gives his messages to the German Embassy in New York and the Germans send coded messages through South America to Germany. What they don't know is that we have broken their code. I have travelled four times between here and New York carrying messages to Devoy and many back. I'm well trusted now. But not enough to get in the IRB inner circle."

I shook my head. "I've never heard of any of these people."

Holmes grinned at me. "You never heard of Moriarty either!"

"Touché," I laughed.

"Well, Watson, let us enter the lion's den."

As we walked to the front door of the building, I saw a

soldierly figure beside it. In the dark, the uniform colour was indistinct but he wore a slouch hat pinned up on one side, like a Boer or Australian and carried an antiquated Mauser rifle. As we approached, he brought his weapon to port arms but then relaxed.

"Ah, it's you, Liam. And how are things at the Castle today?" he said, showing a big grin. "And who is this with you?"

"Sean, this is a friend of mine all the way from San Francisco, America. Came to work with me at the Castle," Holmes said and nudged the man with his elbow. "His name is Thomas Ryan and he's a medical doctor."

"Well, glad I am to meet you, sir," said the guard, extending his hand to shake mine. "Nothing much going on tonight, Liam." He turned toward Holmes. "Just some of the big wigs having another palaver."

"Well, I just want to introduce the doctor around. Thanks, Sean." Sean held open the door as we entered. Inside was a small foyer. "Er, Liam" I said, "is this place always under guard?"

"Yes, Thomas. They're concerned about a raid by the government. But neither Birrell nor Nathan would precipitate such a move. They know there will be bloodshed and neither wants to be responsible."

We entered the main meeting room as some men were leaving an office on the far side. They were joking and smiling and appeared to be in a good frame of mind. I heard one say,

"Ah, it will all work well. Nothing can stop it now." He stopped talking and turned toward us on seeing that his compatriots were looking at something. Seeing the two of us, he approached with a quick step and a smile. "Liam, how are you? No meeting tonight, what brings you out?"

"Mr Connelly," replied Holmes. "may I introduce a friend of mine and Mr Devoy's, Doctor Thomas Ryan from San Francisco?"

Connelly looked me up and down a moment, then extended his hand. "A friend of Devoy's is a friend of ours." I shook his extended hand and nodded. He was of medium build and with a large bushy moustache. Not more than in his late forties I would guess.

"And how was Devoy doing when you last saw him?"

Cold panic ran through my veins. I'd never seen the bloody Devoy! "Well, very well, the last I saw him, but I'm afraid that was three or four years ago." My mind was racing, remembering my Cunard ticket, I continued. "I just came in from Argentina actually. Liam had wired me he was here and that good work was going on. I could afford to come, so I did." I smiled and hoped no one noticed the sweat on my forehead.

"Well, you're a medical doctor, are you?"

"Yes. I've actually taken a job at the military hospital at Dublin Castle. Liam said that would be helpful."

Connolly smiled over his shoulder at his companions. "Oh, Doctor, how rude of me. Let me introduce Mr Padraig

Pearse of the Irish Volunteers. Mr Thomas Clarke, Mr Michael Mallin, my Chief of Staff and Mr Joseph Plunkett. Gentlemen, Dr Thomas Ryan." There was a general round of hellos and handshaking, then Connelly continued. "Tell me, Doctor, do you think America will come into the war on the side of England?"

"How do I know?" I thought. I tried to look concerned for a minute while I searched for an answer. "Well," I finally said, "the Lusitania sinking last year drove most Americans to believing that Germany was indeed the aggressor in this conflict. But most Americans still view this as Europe's problem. They don't want it. If Germany doesn't sink US Flag carriers, I think we'll leave England on her own!"

Connolly looked thoughtful for a moment then grinned at me and patted my shoulder. "Excellent, Doctor. Excellent. I'm afraid, Doctor, we're just on our way to another meeting. Please come back soon so we can talk. Liam, good night." With that they turned to go.

A great sigh of relief shook me as they all departed out the door through which we had entered. As the door closed behind them, Holmes slapped me on the back.

"Sterling job, old fellow. Believed you myself," he whispered. "Now, let's look about."

There was nothing to be seen of an extraordinary nature: assembly room, offices, that sort of thing, until we reached the cellar. Down on one side was a large, locked steel door. "The armoury and explosives," said Holmes. And in a small side room was an antiquated printing press that might have been new forty years ago.

"The government has shut Connolly's newspaper down twice now for sedition," responded Holmes to my silent question. "He uses what he can get."

On the table next to the printing press was a piece of paper. Holmes picked it up.

"The assembly order for the Volunteers for Easter. Assemble at half six in the evening. If only I knew for sure it was the coming rising."

"But Mycroft's information says the day before," I argued.

"Yes, well, they're playing it close to the vest. Shall we go get a bite, Ryan?" He threw the paper back on the table. "I know a wonderful little pub over near Kingsbridge Station. The walk will help you get the lay of the land."

We departed Liberty Hall, into the night. I could feel the fatigue of a long day and the tension of wondering what would come.

Chapter 4

Saturday

15 APR 1916

I was knocked up early the next morning. It was barely half six when Holmes came in my room. "Up with you, Thomas! Martha will have breakfast ready in a few minutes then we're off to Liberty Hall again before the Castle. I go on duty at eight."

By seven, we had eaten and were on our way to Beresford Place. Everything looked different in the daylight and the city bustled with the life of everyday people going about their business. The traffic was that strange combination of push carts, horse-drawn wagons and motor cars that defined the changes of the early part of the century. Liberty Hall was not in the best nor worst part of the city and the early morning sea smell coming from the quays along the Liffey River was brisk and somewhat pleasant. It was a beautiful Saturday morning.

Sean was gone from the night before but the new guard at the hall was just as happy to see Liam Altamont and meet his friend. Passing inside, we made our way back to the office we had seen Connolly and the others come out of the night before. Holmes stepped to the door and knocked. In a moment the door was answered by Mallin. "Ah, Liam. We were just talking about you. Good morning, Doctor. Would you mind if we spoke to Liam alone a moment?"

I smiled and nodded. "I'll just have a seat by the window bench," I said, and the door shut behind them. I looked around the walls and studied the numerous Nationalist posters that covered them. There were also a lot of trade union posters and a bulletin board full of guidance to the members of the ICA. It was no more than a few minutes before the door reopened and Holmes called to me. "Thomas, come in, will you?"

As I entered, Connolly got up from behind his desk and came around to shake my hand.

"We're glad to have your services, Doctor. Liam speaks highly of you. Seems you have some military experience."

I glanced at Holmes. "Yes, not much, some work with the US Army. First in the Modoc War and then in the Dakota's against the Sioux, but by the early 80's I was in San Francisco. That's where I spent most of my time."

Connolly returned to his desk and sat down, indicating for me to take a chair.

"All I can tell you right now, Doctor is that someday we may have need for you. In the meantime I would like you to give me your opinion of the training and status at the Castle once you've had a chance to settle into your duties there. Will you do that for us?"

"Certainly, whatever I can do for the cause."

"Excellent, Doctor. Now I know you have to get to your new duties, so I won't hold you up." He rose from the desk and coming around again, gripped my shoulder. "We are going tonight to a performance of a little play I have written and I'd be delighted if you'd come back tonight with Liam and see it. It will be in the assembly hall."

"Of course, Sir. I'd be honoured. Now I must be off for I'm due at the Castle."

Holmes and I departed the hall and were not far down the street when I thanked him. "I'm glad we spoke of Dr Ryan's biography last night. I remembered he had served but I hadn't remembered where."

"It's not so much in the detail as it is in the consistency, old fellow. I might have been excused for not remembering if it was Sioux or Apache or whatever, as long as it was Indian wars. After all, we only met twice before Chicago." Holmes smiled.

"I take it they brought you in to talk about me?"

"Yes, one more review to see if you were to be trusted. If we could only break into the inner circle, we'd know for sure about the rising."

As we came to the Castle gate we joined a small crowd of people coming to their daily work, a half day for many because it was Saturday. Everyone seemed to know Holmes as he was greeted cheerfully by everyone we passed. The constable waved us over.

"Liam, who might this be with you?"

"Constable Flood, this is Dr Ryan who will be working in the hospital. Come all the way from America to help us out."

"Ah, that's fine, fine. You take good care of our boys,

Doctor."

"I assure you I will do my very best, Constable."

We moved on and in the main foyer Holmes told me to follow him through a number of hallways until we came to a small office merely marked with the number 6 on the door. He opened the door without knocking. Inside was a long table and six chairs, no windows, no pictures, nothing except a bare room. Holmes closed the door behind me and switched on the single overhead light, then pushed a buzzer next to the door.

"Have a seat, Thomas. They'll be with us in a few moments."

"They? Who are they?"

"Major Price of the Army and Detective Sergeant Burns of the DMP."

"I take it you don't care for Burns," I said. "It tells in your voice."

Holmes looked at me out of the corner of his eye. "If it's that telling, I must watch myself."

At that moment, the door opened and two men walked in. The one in uniform was obviously Major Price. The other was in civilian clothes, a fairly expensive, well-tailored suit by the looks of it. He was tall, thin, with brown hair and hazel eyes and wore a perpetual smile which reminded me of someone with *Ricus Sardonicus*.[5] I disliked the man on sight. He was not to be

---

[5] An abnormal, sustained spasm of the facial muscles that appears to produce grinning.

trusted. I looked at Holmes, who I suddenly noticed had been watching my face intently. He smiled and nodded.

"Dr Ryan," said Holmes. "Let me introduce you to Major Price and DS Burns."

We did the obligatory round of handshaking and sat at the table.

"Well, Liam." started the Major. "Anything new?"

"No, unfortunately. The inner circle has continued to meet on a regular basis but that causes its own problem. An increase or decrease in frequency would tell us something. As it is, it tells us nothing. I will say that whatever is going on, I'm convinced that MacNeill, the Volunteer commander, is being kept in the dark by the others. He and Bulmer Hobson are never called to those meetings."

Price turned to me. "And Doctor, what is to be your piece in this affair?"

"As I see it," I replied, "as a medical man, I may have access to people and events that others won't. Anything I find, I will report to, ah, Liam, as quickly as possible. I can also feed information to the Nationalists that you, shall we say, want them to know."

"Good. I understand you're currently an Army doctor?"

"Yes, auxiliary hospital in Kent."

"Seen any action?"

"Before your time, Major," I laughed. "Second Afghan

41

War and Second Boer War."

Price nodded and I smiled to myself. So I'd passed the "what are your credentials" check!

Major Price went on. "We still believe they are planning a rising for Holy Saturday, but we must have more information!" He pounded on the table. Realizing what he had done, he sat back and smiled. "The good news is that Sir Roger's efforts in Germany have been a completely failed. He has but a handful of men." Price went on to review much of what I already knew. In fact, it looked like I knew more than he did for he said nothing about an arms shipment. The whole time Burns appeared to be terribly disinterested. I put it down to the fact that he had heard it all before.

When Price had finished, I told him I hoped I could add to their intelligence data soon and in a concrete way since there was only a week before Holy Saturday.

"I still think this is a tempest in the tea pot," Burns said. They were his first words since we met. "MacNeill won't give up control of the Volunteers and he won't allow a rising. And if we move to take their weapons, he will go for all-out war. But only then."

"You're wrong, Sergeant." It was Holmes. "MacNeill doesn't know it, but he no longer controls the Volunteers, at least not in Dublin. He is going to be as surprised as you will be!"

Price and Burns looked intently at Holmes. "There is something else working," he continued. "I'm convinced that the inner circle is working on releasing a document that will enrage the Volunteers. I don't know the content yet, but it is meant to cause further discontent with the government." Holmes looked directly at Burns. "And you, sir, need to get better informants. Every one of your men is known to the Volunteers and the Brotherhood. The game is being played on both sides."

Burns and Holmes looked at each other with unblinking stare. Burns held his painted smile.

"Whatever is going on, Mr Altamont, it won't cause a rising. They've been turning out their seditious trash for years, to no point."

"This time you're wrong, Sergeant. It's going to be something well thought out and powerful enough to take the kettle to the boil."

Price looked from one man to the other. "Right then, well, we have to explore all avenues." He looked at his watch, one of the newer wrist-watches that had become so popular since the start of the war. "Altamont, you're late for shift. I'll have to write you up again." We laughed and rose. "Liam, you and the doctor leave first. DS Burns and I will wait a few minutes. Doctor," he extended his hand, "here's to a short and successful association."

As we left the room, Holmes pointed me down the hallway. "You're not to report for duty officially until Monday, Thomas. Why don't you spend the day getting to know the city and spend some time back at Liberty Hall. I suspect they'll have more questions for you. Don't forget what we agreed to last night."

"Liam," I started. "This Burns…"

"Later, Thomas. Later." And he was off in the other direction. I was left to find my way.

I first asked directions to the hospital, where I found a well-organized set of wards. I did not make myself known since I did not want to be drawn into a day of handshaking and introductions. That would wait. I decided to take the long way back to Liberty Hall and walk the area as Holmes had suggested. As I left the gate, I waved to Constable Flood, then took out the pocket map of Dublin that Mycroft had seen fit to provide me. It was still early in the day and a long walk would do me good and help clear my head.

On leaving the Castle, I went past the City Hall and proceeded across the Liffey on the Capel Street Bridge. Then I went along the quays and up to the Parkgate by the Royal Barracks, where I made a circle across the river to Kingsbridge Station and then to the Royal Hospital. Phoenix Park was just a short walk from there back across the river, so I walked up the main road through the park. From there I could see the military headquarters, and to the west, the ammunition magazine. A short bit on and on my right was the back of Vice Regal Lodge. I started back toward the main part of town. I was impressed by the vast number of barracks in Dublin, but the lack of men would mean that a large force of rebels could run amuck in the city with the soldiers having to defend so many locations. I sat for a bit on a bench in front of the Ross Hotel, not far from Kingsbridge Station and next to the Royal Barracks. Spreading my map on my knee, I started counting.

I counted at least nine barracks, then there was the Castle to protect, the Vice Regal Lodge, a half-dozen hospitals, seven major railroad stations and yards, the Customs House, and the Bank of Ireland; how in God's name could you protect everything? And if what Holmes had said was true and there were 4,000 volunteers, they outnumbered us. Our only advantage was in weapons.

Somewhat disheartened, I gathered up my map and decided to head for Talbot Street for a bit instead of Liberty Hall. I walked back down along the Liffey until I came to Sackville and walked north toward Earl Street.

As I passed the new General Post Office, I thought, what a beautiful building. It had only recently been renovated and the statues of Hibernia, Mercury and Fidelity stood watch from the top of it. Then I noticed something else - dozens of telephone and telegraph wires. I shook my head. This would have to be defended too. It was a centre of communications and somewhere, I knew, there would be the central lines of the National Telephone Company. It, too, would have to be held. It all seemed impossible.

As I walked east on Earl Street, I continued to ponder. There were troops in Curragh and Athlone but that meant trains. If the countryside rose and they dropped the bridges a half hour train trip might be a day or longer through a hostile countryside. I wondered just how much support these potential rebels had?

By now, I had returned to the rooming house and Mrs

Hudson and I spent a pleasant two hours talking about old times in Baker Street. She assured me that Holmes had not decorated any of her current walls with bullet holes spelling out GR. On finishing lunch I walked a few minutes down to Liberty Hall, determined to stay but a moment and then continue my walk of the city.

As I walked to the front door, I saw that Sean was back on duty and he greeted me as "hail fellow, well met." We were already friends forever.

"Busy lot in there today, Doctor." He leaned forward in a conspiratorial mode. "Mr Connolly and the lot are getting ready for his play tonight. Been rehearsing all week, they have." He leaned back. "Won't be much else going on."

I thanked my new friend, smiled and entered. As I did, I could hear quite a commotion coming from the assembly hall. I entered the hall to a number of looks from people standing about. Others were moving some furniture at the far end of the hall, setting the scenery as it were. Mallin came up to me and shook my hand.

"Back already, Doctor?"

"Yes, I'm not truly due to report until Monday so I decided to walk the city and get my bearings."

"Fine idea. We've got a few boys that know every ally, passage and building. Kind of like those 'Baker Street Irregulars' that Sherlock Holmes fellow had."

Panic screamed in my ears. Was he on to us? Were

Holmes and I being played or was this just an innocent comment?

"Doctor, are you all right?"

"Oh, fine. Fine. I was just thinking about something."

"Come on back to the office," he said, taking my arm. "So you've been to the Castle today? Well maybe you can help me." We entered the empty office and Mallin indicated a couple of empty chairs. "What, Doctor, do you think of the Castle? Pretty solid place, eh?"

I looked at him for a moment. "Mallin, if you're asking me how defensible it is, the answer is very. Solid walks, gates, constables and armed guards and a barrack of about 125 soldiers according to my estimate. There is, of course, the hospital as well. They have food, water and a guard room with a dozen armed soldiers at all times and a supply of ammunition. Is that the answer to your question?"

Mallin looked at me intently before he smiled. "You've a good head on your shoulders, Doctor. I guess you do have some military experience." He leaned back a bit and shrugged. "Of course, this is only for my own personal curiosity, you understand."

"Of course" I smiled and offered him a cigar from my pocket case.

"Well, you're a gentleman, Doctor. I'll say that for you."

We both rose and started out of the office as he was lighting the cigar. "Coming back tonight for the play I hope.

47

Sean Connelly from the Abbot Theatre will be playing the lead role. It's James' first play. I think you'll enjoy it and it'll give me a chance to introduce you around."

I thanked him and assured him I wouldn't miss it for anything. I left, thinking to myself, *exactly what Holmes said would happen, and our rehearsal was much more interesting.*

Having walked the area between the Liffey and the Grand Canal, I returned to Talbot Street about an hour later to find Holmes already there and Mrs McGuffey putting out tea.

"Ryan, you're just in time. I thought you would be back shortly. How was your walk?"

"Enlightening, Holmes."

"Liam."

"Yes, Liam. At any rate, I'm ready for some tea."

"Good, you can fill me in on your thoughts." He commenced pouring the tea as I sat down and started telling him of my discoveries. When I had finished Holmes walked to the window and looked down on the streets.

"You're right, of course, my friend. If there is a full rising and they get their German machine guns, there will be thousands dead, and it will play well for the Germans, as we will have to take troops from France. The end won't be in doubt. Only the cost." He shook his head. "And what of your time at Liberty Hall?"

"I told Mallin exactly what we rehearsed last night. He believes the Castle will be costly to take but I don't believe he's deterred."

"Yes, I was afraid of that. Pity there are only about two dozen soldiers in the whole place." He went back to looking out the window.

"Tell me about Burns," I said.

Holmes turned back from the curtain. "You first, Watson. What can you tell me about him?"

"It's Thomas," I smirked. "Well he makes my skin crawl. You can't trust anyone with such a make-believe smile."

Holmes laughed. "Anything else?"

"Well, he's Protestant, a Unionist and either has a source of income outside his DMP salary or has influential friends."

"Excellent my friend, and how do you know?"

"He had a signet ring with the Freemason crest. I'd recognize it anywhere, as you know, from my army days. Since Catholics or Jews can't join the Masons, he's not either. The suit he wore is well beyond what someone on his pay could afford, so he has separate income or well-placed friends."

"And Unionist?"

"In my travels south of the Liffey this afternoon, I saw him enter the Kildare Street Club, which I'm told is a Unionist stronghold. 'Nationalists need not apply.' At least that's what the tobacconist told me."

"Thomas, you never cease to amaze me! Correct on all counts. It may interest you to know that while the DMP and the

49

RIC have plenty of Catholic constables, the hierarchy is almost exclusively Protestant Unionist. There are one or two exceptions of course. In fact the G-Division men must take an oath to join no secret society except the Freemasons. Their job depends on it. Does that tell you where their loyalties must lie? As you said, 'No Nationalist need apply'."

"I just don't trust that man, Holmes. There's something in the way he looks and carries himself."

"Your intuition does you credit, Thomas, but what is your reasoning?" I shrugged. "You really must learn to think these things out," he continued. "At any rate, I have to agree with you. He has discarded all my warnings and fails to follow up on information which I have been able to supply. He is playing his own game. But as of yet I haven't been able to determine what that game is. I appreciate your confirmation of my ideas."

Holmes filled his pipe and sat across the table. "I have not yet found his source of income but you may like to know that his house would be well beyond the means of most DMP Officers, even sergeants." He fell silent while he drew on his pipe.

My thoughts were racing. Why was the one man most responsible in the police force for listening to us, not doing so? Was he actually a Volunteer and we did not know it? Did he want the rising to occur because he hated the Volunteers and wanted them crushed by violence? Was there a third reason I could not fathom? My thoughts were broken by my friend's voice.

50

"Come, Thomas. We don't want to be late for the world premiere of Mr Connolly's play. He would never forgive us!" Holmes was standing at the door grinning back at me. Grabbing my felt, I was out the door and down the stairs right behind him.

When we arrived back at Liberty Hall it was not yet dark but the building was lighted like a great party was about to take place. People of all classes were gathered about, many in uniform of the ICA. Once again, Liam was well met by everyone. The only other time I had seen my friend display this kind of affability was years ago during the affair of Charles Augustus Milverton. At that time he was attempting to ingratiate himself with one of the parlour maids while in the disguise of a plumber. And that was what, more than 20 years ago?

"Stay by me Thomas, and I'll try to point out some of the key players in 'our drama'."

"Of course, Liam."

Holmes proceeded to point out one important person after another. To this day, I cannot remember all that were there. There were, of course, the men we had met the day before: Mallin, Pearse, Clarke and Plunkett. Holmes pointed to a far corner.

"There's DeValera, the tall one. He's legally an American, but hasn't lived there since the age of two. He's a battalion commander in the Volunteers but has not made it to their inner circle either. He's talking with Willie Pearse, that's Padraig's brother. Willie is a good man but is easily led."

Holmes went on naming names that meant nothing to

me. I finally determined to try and remember faces so I'd at least know which side people were on.

As lights flicked on and off to tell all to take their seats, I noticed a very striking woman up toward the front of the assembly hall.

"Who's that?" I asked.

"Ah, Thomas, leave it to you to always ask about the women!" Holmes smiled out of the side of his mouth. "She's one you need to know. I'll introduce you later." We took our seats for the first scene of the one act play, "Under Which Flag", by James Connolly.

The play was a rather short affair, only three scenes. I will say that Sean Connolly put in an excellent performance as Dan McMahon (a little too alliterative to me). McMahon was a survivor of '48 and stirring up patriotic support for the rising of '67. It wasn't bad but it obviously was meant to raise Irish Nationalist ardour for another rising. The impassioned performance told me exactly where the ICA stood and where it was going.

The play ended with Sean Connolly holding up a green flag and saying something like, "Under this flag only will I serve. Under this flag, if need be, I will die." And the play ended. The crowd rose to their feet and Sean was called back for three curtain calls. Author James Connolly, came forward and held up his hands for quiet. He raised his right hand in the air and looked out over the crowd. "The next act of the play," he said, "will be written by all of us together."

The crowd erupted with cheers. I applauded heartily with the rest and turned to Holmes. "Is he saying what I think?"

"Exactly, Thomas."

As the crowd started to disperse, Holmes brought me forward to meet the woman I had pointed out to him earlier. Spying us approaching she held her hand out to Holmes.

"Altamont, old boy. Good to see you. And who is this gentleman with you? A supporter of the arts?"

"Countess Markievicz, may I present Dr Thomas Ryan, who has come to join the cause."

The countess was a tall woman, thin and while not beautiful, what is called, handsome. She was striking in energy and enthusiasm.

"I am delighted to meet you, Countess."

"I admit I've already heard about you, Doctor. Word gets around quickly here. But if you will excuse me, I must go talk to James. His play was so wonderful, don't you think?"

"Indeed, Madam."

The countess turned to go then evidently thinking of something, turned back to me. Putting a hand on my arm, she said "We may have great need of you, old boy," and walked away.

Holmes and I looked at each other as she disappeared in the crowd. Holmes motioned me to silence and I followed him out to the street.

"I believe it's time for a walk and a pint, Thomas."

"Yes, Liam, I think so."

It was during our walk that Holmes explained the countess' extraordinary position, having founded the Nationalist Boy Scout movement, Fianna Eireann, along with Bulmer Hobson and being an officer in the ICA.

"What? You mean to fight?"

"Yes, Thomas. A great number of women have armed themselves. The Cumann na mBan is the women's organization associated with the Volunteers. They, too, don't just act as secretaries or nurses but many arm themselves as well."

"Amazing," I replied.

"Quite, but we'll talk more about MacNeill, Hobson, and the others I pointed out after our supper."

Chapter 5

Sunday

16 APR 1916

It was a bright, if chilly, Sunday morning. I had been used to rising early at the hospital in Kent and so even without Holmes' knock on the door, I was already up and dressed at seven.

I met Holmes in the sitting room awaiting Mrs McGuffey's fine breakfast and reading the *Irish Times*.

"Ah, Thomas, good. There is not much we can do today. It is my day off and I have a few people I want to visit in the countryside. I'll be taking the train to Cork and won't be back until late. Coffee?"

"No, Liam, I don't think so. You know I'm not a religious type. I haven't been to Mass since I was 14 but for some reason I think I'll go today. St. Mary's has an 8 o'clock Mass."

Holmes looked at me quizzically. "Ah, yes, can't go eat or drink from midnight to go to communion. Well enjoy your walk. It certainly won't hurt your persona with Pearse and crew to be seen there. But, Watson," he said as I reached for my felt, "don't be going rebel on me."

"Ah, Holmes, I assure you that is not a worry."

It was a short walk to St. Mary's and I had plenty of

time, so I diverted first down toward the Custom's house and then along the quays. Dublin was indeed, a beautiful city.

I will admit I felt a little awkward at Mass. It had been fully fifty years since I'd attended church. There was one Mass in a tent in South Africa during the Boer War, but it had been interrupted by some serious shelling.

Like most people, I sat toward the rear of the church. I actually found it somehow comforting that so little had changed in the conduct of the Mass and how well I remembered the Latin responses that had been drilled into me as a child.

When Mass was over, I found myself just outside the railings of St Mary's trying to decide how to best occupy my time.

"You're Doctor Ryan, aren't you?" It was one of the many men I had been introduced to the night before.

"Yes, I am and you are… I'm afraid I met so many people last night I didn't get everyone's name. I'm sorry."

"Pearse, Willie Pearse."

"Yes, of course and your brother is Padraig, is he not?"

"Exactly, everybody remembers Padraig."

"Well I just remember there were two brothers, Willie and Padraig."

"Are you after some breakfast now?" he asked.

"Yes, I was thinking the Gresham Hotel. I'm told they serve a marvellous table. Would you be my guest?"

"I'd be delighted," said Willie. "Let me get my bicycle and I'll walk with you."

"Live a long way from here?"

He pulled his bicycle off the railing. "Yes, a bit of a distance. I'm really not in this parish but I like the pro-cathedral. Especially Father O'Flanagan. So I come here for mass once in a while."

"What do you mean, pro-cathedral?"

"It means provisional cathedral. When the English took St. Patrick's from the Catholics and gave it to the Church of Ireland, the pope never gave up claim to it. When the Irish were once again given the right to have churches, the bishop needed a cathedral but since the government wouldn't give back St. Patrick's, St. Mary's was made the provisional cathedral. The same problem exists for churches all over Ireland."

"How interesting, I had never thought about that. But here we are. Please be my guest. Perhaps you can tell me more about the other sights in the city." Or perhaps, I thought to myself, you can tell me what I really want to know.

We had a delightful breakfast and I found my new friend to be a truly excellent and refined young man. He was kindness itself and he insisted on leaving his bicycle at Liberty Hall and escorting me about the city. We walked mostly to the north of the Liffey up to the Royal Canal and back before collecting his bicycle and having a late lunch back across the river and south to Trinity College.

I especially found interesting Willie's explanation of the importance of the General Post Office. It seems that Sackville Road and the area to the front of the GPO was a common area for speakers and demonstrators, a traditional site of assembly.

Down at Trinity College we were able to enter the library and look about.

"Did you go to school here, Willie?"

"Oh, no, Catholics can't go here. Neither Catholics nor Jews. It's legal now, but it's understood we're not wanted."

I put that in the back of my mind. Another case of separation. No wonder we had problems. It was near four o'clock when we parted and I thanked Willie profusely for his kindness. We shook hands and I watched him ride off down past Trinity and I turned to re-cross the river.

I supped alone that night then decided to visit our favoured pub. It was a fountain of information for those who wished to listen. I was given a pint of Guinness without having to ask and stood near the end of the bar.

The talk around me was general - the war, a job open at the brewery, cost of or lack of petrol, but here and there in corners sat men I had seen at Liberty Hall. They were deep in conversation.

It was close to nine and I was about to leave when Holmes walked in. "Thomas, will you share a pint?" We took our glasses and went to a table near the windows. The place had thinned out considerably and we talked quietly.

"Interesting trip?" I asked.

Holmes looked at his glass. "Yes and no. I went to Cork to see what I could find out. If there is to be a rising, none of the rank and file know anything. And their battalion commander gives the impression of one who suspects something but isn't sure. I tell you, Thomas, they've kept the date well hidden. Everything tells me Easter Sunday night, which goes against our intercept information of Holy Saturday. It's absolutely frustrating."

We sat for some time while Holmes smoked his pipe and I another cigar. Finally, he rose. "Well, Thomas, tomorrow is another day. Shall we be off?"

As we walked back to Mrs McGuffey's, I related all I had done for the day. I now felt I knew the main roads and thoroughfares and the principle buildings.

"Holmes, if they put 4,000 armed men in the field, they can overwhelm each outpost one at a time and take the whole city. That is, if the countryside rises too."

"Yes, Watson, I know. But Nathan won't move without more proof. So we must get it for him. Tonight however, a good rest. You, my friend, start work at the Castle tomorrow and must report early."

Chapter 6

Monday

17 April 1916

Holmes and I walked to Dublin Castle that Monday morning so as to arrive in good time. His parting advice to me as we went our separate ways at the gate was to concentrate on my duties, but to keep my ears open. Information could come from anywhere.

The hospital was actually in very pleasant surroundings. State apartments at the Castle had been taken over by the Red Cross and supplemented the city and government hospitals in the case of wounded coming home from the continent.

As a Red Cross hospital, much of the funding came from subscriptions. In fact, where regular hospitals received 4 shillings a day for each bed occupied, our hospital received only 3 shillings even though the actual cost was 3 shillings 11 pence.

But the hospital was well equipped to care for 250 men at a time. Another 50 could be taken care of in open air verandas. As it was, on the day I reported there were 182 beds occupied. Most of the wounded were those who might, with good care, return to duty in a few months. Some I knew would never return to duty but would have to be issued their silver badge. A few, I could tell, would have to go to a facility like the one I had just come from.

All the doctors and nurses were Red Cross volunteers and so, while paid, received far less than their services were worth. They worked for the good of the soldiers.

For my first day, we started with a tour of the "wards" and a discussion of our capabilities. I was very pleased with what I found, to include radiographs and a well-equipped surgery. I was assigned a case load by the senior surgeon and before I knew it, six o'clock had come. The doctors took turns spending the night on-call at the hospital but it was decided I would work a week before being assigned to the duty roster.

The one advantage to this hospital was that there was no daily intake. The bad thing was that patients came in boat-loads. About once a month the hospital ship, Oxfordshire, would appear in Dublin harbour with 900 or more men in need of help. From Dublin Harbour, the Irish Automobile Club Ambulance Service, R.A.M.C. and St. John's Ambulance Brigade would distribute the men throughout the city hospitals or take them to special trains to Belfast. Knowing that Holmes was by now off duty, I started for the gate when I was tapped on the shoulder. It was Holmes. He said nothing but walked past me and headed for Room 6. This time, when we entered the room, it was filled with people.

Mr Nathan looked up from his place at the head of the table, nodded and indicated two empty chairs.

"Gentlemen," said Nathan. "Let me introduce Mr Altamont, and I assume, this is Dr Ryan, both of Special

Branch. I believe, Mr Altamont, you know everyone. Doctor, you know the Major and DS Burns. This is Mr Edgeworth-Johnstone, head of the DMP and Sir Neville Chamberlain, head of the RIC. We have much to discuss, so we best get about it."

I drew in a little as I sat. Surely Chamberlain wouldn't recognize me. We had spent three days next to each other in hospital after the siege of Kandahar, but that was some 35 years ago. He looked at me, then at Holmes as we took our seats. There was no spark of recognition.

"Major Price, if you will start."

"Of course, sir. There has been no significant change to our current situation. The Volunteers continue to make noise, interfere with recruiting and give speeches. Their parade on St. Patrick's Day gave us a chance to count men and weapons. It appears that they have over 13,000 men at this point but if you discount shotguns, they've probably got no more than 3,000 serviceable rifles of various types. The rumours continue about a rising in conjunction with the manoeuvres on Easter weekend but we have been unable to confirm this."

"Thank you," said Nathan. "I have a letter to share with you gentlemen. It comes to us from our Army commander in the south. He contends that the Navy has told him that they expect a landing of weapons by the Germans on our South West Coast and that they believe there is a rising planned for Holy Saturday. The Navy also says that Sir Roger Casement is on his way to lead the rising. What the Navy won't do is tell us how they know all this. Comments, Gentlemen?"

Everyone looked around the table. Holmes caught my eye and shook his head as if to say, "say nothing".

"Mr Edgeworth-Johnstone," continued Nathan, "Comments?"

The head of the DMP looked at the table for a moment and then at Burns. "As you know, Undersecretary, we have numerous avenues of information. None of these avenues have brought us an iota of viable information that would lead me to believe that a revolt is imminent. Why it would be preposterous," he blustered. "No rising by a few rebels could ever succeed and MacNeill knows that. He won't let it happen."

Nathan nodded. He turned to Chamberlain. "And the RIC's position?"

"Like the DMP," he said, nodding across the table. "We have numerous informants throughout the island. The Volunteers have been good at marching about. But a rising? Surely not. Though," he continued, a little uncomfortably, "I would like to know where the Navy is getting it's information."

"Mr Burns, would you like to contribute?" asked Nathan.

"As you all know, the Volunteers are riddled with our informers, all men whom I trust and are well placed. There has been no unusual activity either at Dawson Street or at Liberty Hall for the last month. I'll admit we have not been able to penetrate the IRB meetings at Clark's Tobacco shop but neither have our colleagues from Special Branch. Or have you, Mr Altamont?"

Everyone turned to look at Holmes.

"No sir, I have not. But let me assure you of this," Holmes leaned forward over the table. "I have been at Liberty Hall for the last two hours. The men who intend to lead this rising have been there also, sequestered in Connolly's office. Their mood is one of excitement. They have been working on the wording of some documents. One, I believe, they will release fairly soon. The other, I believe to be a Declaration of Independence, to be read at the start of the uprising. These men won't be stopped by MacNeill or anyone else. It will start this weekend and you need to confine all the King's forces to barracks to be ready to deal with the rising when it comes." Holmes leaned back in his chair, his right hand drumming on the table. Everyone was silent.

Burns was the first to speak. "Gentlemen, I completely and wholeheartedly disagree with Mr Altamont. If there were going to be a rising, I would know of it!"

"Forgive me, sir," said Nathan, looking at Burns. "This is not rivalry or pride speaking? You are convinced?"

"Yes, sir. I raise my right hand, and as God is my witness, there will be no rising."

"Well," continued Nathan, "Mr Altamont, I appreciate your input. But for now I must defer to the DMP. Major see if you can find out where the Navy is getting their information. I think that will be all for now. We'll meet again when we have more information."

With that, we dispersed. Holmes held me back in a

corner of the hallway for a moment. By now it was almost half seven and dark outside.

"Should we get something to eat?" I asked.

"No, Thomas, I have a belief our friend Burns somehow intends to profit from this rising. I don't know how yet, but I will. We're going to follow him. I want to know more about him."

We stayed a good block back from our prey and followed as he crossed the river and headed for the Brunswick Street Police Station. As we trailed along, I mentioned to Holmes that I had known Chamberlain in Afghanistan.

"He gave no sign of recognition."

"No, Liam. It's been too long ago. He might remember the name Dr Watson, but I'm sure he didn't recognize me."

"He's the man who brought you and Thurston together, wasn't he?"

"What?"

"Invented the game snooker, didn't he?"

I had to admit he had and Thurston and I had spent many hours playing it at the club.

We had taken up a position in a doorway down the street where we could watch the entrance to the police station. We didn't have to watch long as in about fifteen minutes, he came out and headed east. Soon we were re-crossing the river and headed down near Trinity College and on to St. Stephen's

Green. South of the green he came up to a group of six men standing near an alleyway. They all nodded as Burns approached and followed him down the alley. As they disappeared, we hurried to the top of the alley just in time to see the last one go through a red painted door, in what appeared to be a small warehouse.

"What now?" I asked Holmes.

"Now, we get your supper, Thomas. I've seen exactly what I want."

"And that was?"

"Later, Thomas. Later."

"Holmes, you are insufferable!"

He merely smiled and headed north up the street. "Were you able to overhear any more at Liberty Hall than you told Nathan?"

Holmes looked frustrated. "It's as I told them. They are preparing a declaration of independence. I distinctly heard Connolly demanding the inclusion of the equality of women in the document."

"Could it be just some general statement?"

"No, I assure you, it's more." He was quiet for a moment as we walked along. "I also heard Plunkett call Pearse, Mr President. Watson, they are forming a government and if the fools in Dublin Castle won't act, then they will be responsible for the coming bloodshed."

We continued a bit in silence.

"What of those men with Burns?" I finally asked.

"All in good time, Thomas. All in good time."

Chapter 7

Tuesday

18 April 1916

Tuesday was to be another disappointing day. Early once again, Holmes and I went to Liberty Hall but finding no one save the guard we walked down to Volunteer Headquarters. There Padraig Pearse was already in attendance and welcomed us warmly. Sean Fitzgibbon and a few others were about and Pearse was writing at his back desk when we arrived.

"Good morning, Liam, Doctor," he called from the chair. Getting up he handed two notes to Fitzgibbon. "You'll have to hurry Sean if you're to make the train."

Fitzgibbon seemed uncomfortable, fidgeted for a moment, looked up at Holmes and me and departed.

"What brings you gentlemen out so early?"

"Just checkin' to see what needs doin' Mr Pearse." It was Holmes's tolerable accent.

"I've never really thanked you properly, Liam, for all you've done. Your trips back and forth across the Atlantic to Mr Devoy have been a great help. Someday you'll know how much." He started walking back to his desk. "But right now I don't have anything of consequence going on."

"C'mon Mr Pearse, somethin' is goin' on. Everybody runnin' around like they are!? And all that hustle at the Castle?

Somethin's up."

"No, Liam. Just the usual scurry when we're getting ready for manoeuvres. But what's happening at the Castle?"

"They've got the wind up over somthin'. DMP, RIC, Military Intelligence seems to be meeting quite a bit. Don't know why."

"Liam, it's important that you try to find out what you can. You know there is a real danger that they may come for our weapons. If so, I need warning of it."

As we were leaving the room, Pearse reiterated, "Remember Liam, anything you hear might be useful."

We hustled out onto Dawson Street and made straight away for the Castle, reaching there barely in time to start shift.

I was once again completely occupied for the day, not even breaking to eat but a mouthful at lunch.

It was after six when I made my way back to Mrs McGuffey's. There I found Holmes in the sitting room staring out the windows. The room was filled with smoke. It was suffocating.

"Holmes, do open a window," I gasped.

"Ah, Thomas, yes, go ahead if you wish." He left the window and sat at the table while I threw up the sash.

Holmes was in the midst of re-charging his pipe when I sat down.

"Your patients are doing well, I trust?"

"Yes, quite a fine group of men. I've referred a couple for special treatment, hysteric cases, but for the most part, they're doing well." I got some water from a carafe that was kept on the side table. "And you, Holmes? Is this a three-pipe problem?"

Holmes smiled and tossed a match on the table. "Thomas, I had another round with our know-nothing friends today. Lord Wimbourne, the Lord Lieutenant, is back from England. He called a meeting at the Viceregal Lodge with Nathan and Chamberlain. They went over the information from the Navy. Weapons are on the way and there is to be a rising on Holy Saturday. But since the information is second hand and not straight from the War Department, they refuse to listen. They then called in Burns who said, "If there were to be a rising, I would know" again! Even Major Price recommended waiting. Watson, they could end all this with a midnight roundup of a dozen men. Instead, we must get them more proof."

"Holmes, you can't expect them to just take your word for it."

"I suppose not," said Holmes and retired into one of his blue funks. I waited for a few moments.

"Liam, I'm famished. Shall we get something to eat?"

"Yes, well, we might as well. Usual place I suppose." He tapped his pipe out on the table, grabbed his cap and we went down the stairs to the street. As we came out on the darkening sidewalk, Holmes suddenly grabbed my arm and pulled me back into the doorway.

"What?" I started.

"Hush! Look, over there, on the other side of the street. The man walking west in the felt."

"Why, it's one of the men Burns met last night. You couldn't miss that hat."

"Let's follow him, Watson."

So we did, down Earl to Sackville, across the bridge to College Street Police Station, where he entered. We waited a bit down the street.

"Hol.... Liam, do you know who that man is?"

"Yes, Thomas. His name is Dowdle. He's one of Burns' informants. More than that, he's a cracksman[6] with an extensive history. He's been fairly active of late, but for some reason, all the cases against him fall apart. I'm sure you can guess why."

"Too valuable to Burns as an informant," I responded.

"That, too," said Holmes.

I was about to ask what he meant when Dowdle came out of the station.

"Thomas, I think we're going to a different pub tonight. The same one as Mr Dowdle." With that, we were back off in pursuit.

Dowdle led us to a small pub in the Temple Bar district. We let him precede us by a good five minutes, then entered.

---

[6] Safe cracker.

Dowdle was seated at a table on the far side of the room with two other men. They didn't look up as we entered but leaned in together over the table, intent in conversation. Holmes and I sat near the door and ordered food and a pint.

The drinks came and we sat in silence, sipping the brown stout. I found I was actually acquiring a taste for the stuff. Our food came and still Dowdle and his two companions were in close conversation. I had just started to eat when two more men came through the door to meet with Dowdle. The five men crowded around to the point where their heads must have been touching. They whispered to each other. I couldn't help but think of a comic scene in a bad play.

"Liam," I mimicked our friends in the corner, leaning close to Holmes. "Those are all the same men from last night, aren't they?"

"Yes. Only one missing, plus Burns."

"Do you know any of the rest besides Dowdle?"

"I do. The first two men who were with Dowdle are petty crooks named Murdock and Simple. I believe the other two are called Johnny Pepper and Phil Conarchy, both of whom are in the ranks of the Volunteers but hold no real position. And both are suspected of a number of burglaries in Rathmine. Actually, I gave Burns all the proof required to arrest Pepper of three separate burglaries."

As we ordered another pint, the men at the table started to leave - first Murdock and Simple, then a few minutes later, Pepper and Conarchy. Dowdle sat back in his chair. He was sitting so that he was looking toward the bar and having been lost in conversation until now, had not looked around to notice us.

As the door opened again, a man of middle height with a cloth cap and overcoat came in. Holmes leaned over and whispered, "Harry Malcolm. A competitor of Dowdle's."

Spying Dowdle, Malcolm went straight to his table where he was greeted as a long, lost friend.

"Not a competitor now," I smiled.

"Yes, Thomas, our sixth man. I now know what is going on. Or at least I believe I do. I think it's time we left It's almost last order and you have an early morning."

We paid for our food and stout and left the two conspirators sitting at their table.

Holmes walked silently for a while and when I could no longer stand it, I blurted out, "Well, what are they going to do?"

"I don't really have enough proof, Thomas," he smiled. "And you know how I love dramatic endings. But put your mind to it. Surely you will come up with the answer. If not, I will explain in good time."

He fell back into silence. The most logical thing I could think of as we approached Talbot Street, was that Burns intended to use these thieves cum Volunteers, to somehow hurt the organization from within, or discredit it to the point where they could gain no popular support.

We had reached Mrs McGuffey's and I was opening the

door when I heard Holmes call out in a loud voice, "Good Night, Mr Dowdle." I looked at Holmes then in the direction he gazed. A hundred yards back stood Dowdle under a street lamp. He approached until he was but a few inches from Holmes.

"I know who and what you are, Altamont! You try to interfere with me and I'll expose you to all."

"Please do so. It will make my task all the easier." They stared at each other. Dowdle was the first to flinch.

"Remember what I said," Dowdle finally murmured, stepping back.

"Your plan counts on me continuing to be unknown. You'll say nothing. Remind your boss at the DMP. Got it, mister?"

Dowdle's fists doubled up and for a moment I thought he would strike Holmes. Silently he turned and walked away. We watched until he turned the corner.

"Holmes, what is going on?"

"Not yet, Watson, not yet." And he went up the stairs.

Chapter 8

Wednesday

19 April 1916

It was now becoming difficult to be both a doctor at the Red Cross hospital and a spy. I felt the next two days things would move swiftly, and I was correct. Holmes left about half seven for the Castle and asked me to go by Liberty Hall for an hour. I had re-arranged my rounds so that I was not due in until ten and would work until six.

When I arrived at the Hall, Connelly was speaking to one of the ICA members, a man by the name of Robert Cacy. I knew Cacy was a trusted ICA man who had been there during the troubles of '13. He was known for both his loyalty and his love of poteen[7]. It was the second issue which kept him from rising higher in the organization. They broke up as I approached and Connolly wished me good morning.

Cacy was more voluble and asked if I'd care for a walk with him. He held a large folder full of papers and was off to deliver them. I accepted his offer thinking "here is a man that is always about, perhaps he has picked up some information he would unwittingly share".

"Surely," I replied after a moment's hesitation. "Where are we off to?"

"I'm to deliver this package to Mr MacNeill and wait to

---

[7] Alcohol usually made illicitly in small quantities from potatoes.

see if he has a response. I'm glad of someone to walk with. They're constantly sending me here and there and never a bit of company."

As we walked I tried to lead the conversation to the upcoming manoeuvres and the ICA's role in them with the Volunteers. My companion, it seemed though, was a dearth of information. If there was something to be known about hurling matches or the GAA, he was your man. But as far as the inner workings of the organization he belonged to, all he wanted to know was that Jim Larkin or James Connolly wanted something done, so he did it. It wasn't that he was unintelligent. He had thought things through, made a decision to follow these two, and he stuck to it. I had to admire him in a way.

When we arrived at MacNeill's it was he who answered the door and asked us in. Cacy presented him with the package and waited dutifully.

"Doctor," said MacNeill, tossing the package on the table, "would you and Mr Cacy care for some coffee?"

Cacy spoke up first. "Aye, Sir. But Mr Connolly says Mr Clarke wants you to read that straight away and I'm to bring back any response, so I am."

MacNeill smiled and picked up the package to unwrap it. "Coffee is on the sideboard, gentlemen. Please help yourselves." He sat at the table taking out papers. As Cacy and I took cups, he started reading and I could see he was becoming greatly agitated. He looked at me with a puzzled face. "Doctor, do you know what's in this?"

76

"No, Sir. I do not."

"Please, come here and read this. I want your opinion."

Putting down my cup, I took the top few papers from his hand. As I did, he started unfolding a map. I read the top paper with utter disbelief. How could this be? A document from the Castle proposing the arrest of all the Nationalist leaders and the possible execution of MacNeill himself! I read on. The document was a copy of an order from a secret file in Dublin Castle. The document was what I would have called a "warning order," i.e.: get ready but don't act until told to do so. It was to be carried out once signed by Sir Matthew and General Friend.

At first I thought the whole thing incredible: The DMP to be confined to barracks, the Army to take up patrols and stand pickets in the street, the Catholic Archbishop's house to be surrounded, whole groups to be arrested and houses and locations to be searched for arms. None of this seemed like Nathan.

But then I began to think. If I were the Army and in this same situation, would I not have such a plan? Wouldn't prudence demand such a plan? Not only dealing with the Nationalists, I'd also have one to deal with the Unionists. It seemed quite reasonable. MacNeill's voice brought me back to the moment. "Well, Doctor, your opinion?"

"I suppose this document could be real," I started. My mind was racing. How to play this? "But of course it purports to be a copy of a document. How close is it to the original, I wonder? And another question, is it for imminent use or a planning exercise?"

"Both good questions, Doctor. This makes no sense. They would be asking for blood to run in the streets. Surely General Friend doesn't mean to arrest leaders, confiscate only Volunteer arms, raid Liberty Hall and Fr. Matthew Park!"

"General Friend isn't even in the country, Mr MacNeill."

"What does it all mean? Mr Cacy, would you inform Mr Pearse I desire a meeting of the executive council at five o'clock? Tell him it is imperative that all are here." MacNeill looked tired and indecisive. "Doctor, we've had rumours about these plans for a few weeks but I didn't know they were so complete. I'd appreciate it if you would return tonight also. A third opinion may be useful." He smiled as if to himself and Cacy and I left him sitting in his chair, shaking his head. Cacy went to find Pearse and I hastened to the hospital.

On arriving at the Castle, I sent an orderly to the telegraph office with a note asking Holmes to meet me as soon as possible. The orderly had no more than returned when I was asked to attend an accident patient in Room 6. Knowing what it must be, I discouraged taking any help and left the wards to meet with Holmes.

When I entered Room 6, I also found Major Price who appeared in a most serious mood. "Thomas," said Holmes, "is this about the Castle document?"

"Oh, you already know," I replied, disappointed. It seemed I could never get one up on Holmes.

"We've heard about it but not seen it yet. I understood Alderman Tom Kelly, of the Dublin Corporation, is even now reading a copy to the corporation and demanding answers. What do you know?"

I proceeded to tell Holmes and Price everything I knew about the document and about my discussion with MacNeill. I ended by asking Price if the document was real.

"From what you tell me, Doctor, I can say the document is a forgery."

Holmes looked him directly in the eye. "But most of it is accurate, is it not, Major?" The Major looked uncomfortable.

"Certainly there are aspects which are accurate. We would be a poor Army indeed if we did not plan for contingencies. But I assure you that such things as surrounding the Archbishop's house are ludicrous. This document has, shall we say, been enhanced."

"You say MacNeill wanted you back with him for the meeting?" asked Holmes.

"Yes, at five."

"I shall go with you. Hmm, what have we here?" Holmes was looking out the window. I went to join him. Below on the street I could see Connolly and Mallin. Connolly was pointing toward one of the Castle gates and Mallin was writing on a pad of paper. "I believe, Thomas, that Mr Connolly is making a last reconnaissance. "

"Mr Altamont," said Price, "I still believe that there will

be no rising. Why even this fallacious document won't cause an armed conflict. It may be bogus, and it may rile them, but it would also put them on notice that there is a plan of action and so further deter them."

"You're wrong," said Holmes. "It will not cause a rising, but it makes it more likely. The Nationalists have always contended that the English do nothing but plot against the Irish and this will help confirm it."

"Thomas, you had best get back to your duties and I will meet you at the gate at four thirty. I'm sure the Major will arrange to have need of you on an errand of some importance so you can leave early. Correct, Major?"

"Of course."

So we broke up and I went back to the wards that I was beginning to feel I was neglecting. At half four, I was once again called back to help Major Price, but this time out in the city. Meeting Holmes just outside the gate, we headed for MacNeill's.

"Have there been any more developments?" I asked as we walked along.

"We were able to get Alderman Kelly's copy of the document," he responded, "and it appears it is a mixture of truth and falsehood, with enough truth to make it believable."

"Will the Castle refute it?"

"Yes, Nathan says he will but Burns has convinced him to wait for the moment to give time to prepare an adequate response."

"Ordinarily I would say that was reasonable, Liam. But to wait may lend credence. They must refute it now."

"I agree," said Holmes, "but as you know, Burns has his own motives for delay. Every moment now to him is critical."

"No, Liam, I don't know." I'm sure the frustration came through in my voice. "Why is delay critical?"

"Come, Thomas, surely you must have a hint of what his game is? No? Well think about it, man." He looked at me, out of the corner of his eye. "All right, I'll give you this: What do Trinity College, Dublin Castle and Castle Street Police Station have in common?" He paused. "And what services do Burns' men provide? You should have the answers." We walked on a few moments. "Here we are, Thomas. Looks as though there is everyone of any importance here." Three motor cars were parked in front of MacNeill's and I could see Pearse's bicycle leaned up against the railing.

As we entered, we saw the room was truly filled with a Who's Who of the Volunteers. "If Price were to strike now, all he'd miss would be Clarke," whispered Holmes.

"Come in, gentlemen, come in," said MacNeill. The chairs all taken, Holmes and I stood in a corner to listen. I knew almost all there. Besides Pearse there was the O'Rahilly, MacDonagh, Joe Plunkett, Ceannt, Bulmer Hobson and others I knew by face but not name. Hobson and the O'Rahilly I knew were moderates and the most trusted by MacNeill. Pearse was his favourite, though, and Pearse was the most radical among them -well, except for Tom Clarke, and Clarke would never be acceptable to MacNeill.

Holmes now knew who the IRB men were and had warned me. MacDiarmada, MacDonagh, Ceannt, Pearse and Plunkett were all IRB and we assumed part of the plan. Hobson, the O'Rahilly and, of course, MacNeill, were not. The last three were the ones being played.

MacNeill started the meeting with a discussion of the Castle document and went through the order in detail.

"It can only mean that the English are set to move against us, quickly," piped up Plunkett as soon as MacNeill had stopped speaking. He was visibly excited. Plunkett was the son of a Papal Count, and part of a Nationalist family. There were no divided loyalties in his world. It was independence or nothing.

Pearse played a good game. He and the others of the IRB got all the concessions from MacNeill that were needed. They all agreed with MacNeill, oh yes, they would only fight if they were attacked. They would preserve their arms and ammunition and defend the organization, but only if the government fired the first shot. It was even MacNeill who recommended that the Volunteers buy supplies of food and medical stores and oil their weapons.

When the meeting broke up, the IRB men could barely hide their emotions of glee. Pearse nearly raced from the house. Hobson and the O'Rahilly hung back a bit and wanted to talk to MacNeill but he insisted he needed some time and so we all left.

Holmes asked Hobson if we could meet him in an hour at Volunteer Headquarters and he agreed. Holmes was exceedingly quiet as we sat at the pub. I ate a little and sipped my pint while he smoked.

At fifteen minutes before eight we started to our meeting.

Holmes startled me when he finally spoke. "They'll strike, no matter what happens, Thomas. The IRB's badly using MacNeill but they believe completely in their cause. To them, a small lie to gain a free Ireland is a small price. They are literally willing to give all, including their lives for what they believe is a great cause. You have to admire them. And who knows, perhaps they're right." He stopped and tapped his pipe out on a railing. "Nonetheless, Thomas, it's our job to stop them. I don't see much hope but perhaps we can convince Hobson and he can convince MacNeill. If they'll cancel the manoeuvres, we may at least delay the bloodshed."

We found Hobson in his office with Captain O'Connell. They were looking rather forlorn.

"Yes, Liam, what did you and the Doctor want to talk about?"

"It's about the Castle document, sir." Holmes went on to explain our concerns: the wording, the irrational sequestering of the DMP, surrounding the Archbishop's house, and the rest. He went on for a good ten minutes attributing his military objections to me and my Indian War campaign. When he finished, both men sat quietly for a moment, then O'Connell

83

said, "It's Plunkett, man. He's taken some of the truth and made it worse. I can't prove it, but I know it."

"It's a wicked conspiracy to force a rising. You can be sure Clarke is behind it," replied Hobson. "We must go see MacNeill. There's more to these manoeuvres than just practice. I can feel it."

We left Hobson and O'Connell putting on their hats and coats for a return to MacNeill as Holmes and I departed for Liberty Hall.

"Let us hope, Watson, that they can get MacNeill to take some action, though I don't hold out much hope."

At Liberty Hall, we found the ICA alone for a change. They were having a drill night and Connolly was having a meeting with Mallin and three of his officers in his office. There was little to be learned here at the moment. It being late, we returned to Mrs McGuffey's.

Chapter 9

Holy Thursday

20 April 1916

I was now feeling that my taking a position at the Red Cross Hospital had been an error. I could not spend the time I thought I needed to gathering information. But it had been a way into the cause. Seen as useful by the Volunteers, Holmes spent time in the telegraph office I thought might be wasted.

Sir Matthew had issued a repudiation of the Castle document the night before and I was curious if it had any impact on MacNeill. We were now only two days from the planned rising and we were no nearer to verifying it. I knew it was to happen, so did Holmes, but without solid proof, it was just so much more talk. At least Holmes had convinced Sir Matthew to issue an alert to the DMP of possible trouble. Our friend Burns, of course, had objected most strenuously.

At four o'clock, I was once again sent for and reported to Room 6. Nathan, Burns, Price and Holmes were all present when I got there.

"Ah, Doctor, we can start." It was Nathan who led off the conversation. "I've had a report by an informer in B Company of the Volunteers that there is something to happen on Easter as opposed to Holy Saturday. Unfortunately, he can't say what. My question to you, gentlemen, is are we or are we not going to see a rising?"

Burns was the first to speak. "Absolutely not," he blurted out. "If there was a rising, I would know." With that, he slapped the table and folded his arms.

Poor Nathan looked rather stunned, but turned to Price. "Major, your opinion?"

"I don't know Sir. We believe that arms are on the way and the Navy has stepped up patrols along the coast to intercept. We also believe that Sir Roger is en route, but again, we've no certainty. If both of these things are true, that combined with the manoeuvres planned for this weekend can't be coincidental. However, I can't be certain."

"Mr Altamont?"

"There will be a rising!"

"How can you be sure?"

"Let me say that MacNeill, the Volunteer leader, has no knowledge of the rising. He's a good man and will only fight if attacked. But don't doubt he's for independence! The IRB will use the Volunteers and the ICA to start a rising this weekend. I guarantee it. The timing is what I lack."

"Where's your proof?" spat Burns, his eyes glaring.

"I admit I have nothing in a concrete form not a letter or an order, nor even an overheard conversation."

"Ha!" cried Burns.

Holmes turned to Sir Matthew. "If you do not take all the leaders, all at once, by Monday there will be a revolution. I believe the Navy reports."

Holmes was playing a two sided game here. He knew that the Navy had broken the German codes and was aware of the arms shipment. He also knew that neither the Army, nor the Irish government, had been told anything official by the Navy for fear of compromising their position and the Germans realizing their codes had been broken. Admiral Bayly in Queenstown had "hinted" to General Stafford about what was happening but the Army had no sources to confirm the "hints".

The air was now still. "Well Gentlemen," said Nathan. "I will not act without proof that can be taken to a court of law. Bring me that and I will act."

"Then, sir," said Holmes, "Burns will have his revolution." The two of us left the room as Burns started a tirade against us.

"Come, Thomas, we've been invited to the Countess's for tea and we must grab a trolley."

As we rode the trolley south toward Rathmine, I asked Holmes why he did not go back to Liberty Hall and look for more proof.

"Because, even though I'm considered a friend and Clan Na Gael, Irish Americans are still somewhat outsiders. However, at the Countess's, we might be able to pick up the conversation we need in an unguarded moment. After all, she and about twenty other women are actually members of the ICA. Connolly is very progressive."

As we rode south, I noticed a motor car which seemed to be moving with the trolley. It would pull ahead each time the trolley stopped and would pull over to the kerb then start up again once we had passed.

"Yes, it's two of the six." It was Holmes. He had been watching me watch the motor car.

"What should we do?" I asked.

"Nothing. Let them stay with us. They are harmless where they are."

"Why doesn't Burns just give us away to the Volunteers? I mean, if it's like you say, and he wants the rising, why not just turn us over?"

"Because, if he does, it may all be called off. They won't know how much we know, so how can they be sure their plans are not already known? He would chance losing his opportunity."

"Holmes, you are frustrating! Opportunity for what?"

"Is it possible you still do not see? Let me expand my clue. What do College Street Police Station, Trinity College, Dublin Castle and the City Hall, and the telephone exchange all see in common?"

With that, he would say no more until we reached Rathmine.

When we arrived, we were welcomed like old friends of the family. We were brought to the countess who was in the dining room with other guests.

"Oh, you'll introduce yourselves in a moment, old dear." She said, taking my hand. "But right now we have great need of you. Doctor, grab that edge of the bed sheet over there and pull it taut. Mr Altamont, keep stirring this pot. It's my own mixture, gold paint and mustard. All I could find, I'm afraid. You must keep it stirred."

She had a green sheet spread across the dining table and four guests held the corners tight while she, with Holmes stirring the pot, wrote in great letters, Irish Republic. All the while she talked of the future face of Ireland, women's suffrage and the like, while a brown cocker spaniel ran at her feet.

I must say, I found the Countess somehow intimidating. She was excited, alive, outspoken and a true equalitarian. I was completely fascinated.

With the new flag drying in the pantry, we had tea and the countess insisted on knowing all about the Indian Wars in America. I cursed myself for not having spent more time reading up on what I had done. I vaguely remembered a few of Ryan's old tales of the Modoc War and what I didn't know, I filled in with what seemed reasonable.

Holmes tried to move the conversation to the ICA and the Volunteers, but while she was expansive on politics she was silent on any action to be taken. In an hour Holmes and I were taking our leave as the Countess had a meeting at Liberty Hall to get ready for.

As we left the Countess's, the same motor car sat a block away. Holmes and I caught a passing trolley and our friends continued their leap frogging.

Having crossed O'Connell Bridge we got off and walked east on the quays toward Liberty Hall. The motor car drove on.

At Liberty Hall we found Sean on guard again. "Hello, Sean, all quiet tonight, eh, no drill?" asked Holmes.

"Not tonight, but lots going on I guess. People been coming and going all afternoon. Robert's just back from Cork. He's inside." I offered Sean a cigar which he took and slipped in his pocket with a "Thank You, Doctor. I'll be using it later."

As we entered the hall, I could see Cacy sitting on one of the benches near Connolly's office. He looked up from his pipe as we approached.

"Been busy, Robert?" asked Holmes.

"That I have. Yesterday they have me all over the country delivering papers from Mr Plunkett's house and today it's Cork and back and a 'hang on a bit, Robert, we've more for you'. You'd think I had nothing of me own to do."

I looked at Holmes and he nodded. So it was Plunkett who printed the Castle document! Holmes sat next to him on the bench and started charging his pipe. "Why to Cork, Robert?"

"I'm sure I don't know now. It's just take this here, and take that there. I never look. A gentleman doesn't look at another's message, ya know!" He pointed empathically with his pipe stem.

"You're right, of course. I wasn't saying you would."

We smoked for a while with Cacy when Holmes looked at his watch. "Doctor, you ready for a pint? Good, then we're gone. See you later, Robert." And we started for our favourite pub.

"Holmes," I finally said, "you really have to work on the accent." It was then I felt the blow to my head and I sprawled across the pavement. It was now quite dark and the attack had come from the shadows. I rolled over on my left side but as I did I received a kick to the stomach. I heard someone shout, "Some help here!" and the attack on me ceased for a moment. I could now see two attackers trying to pin Holmes against the wall and punching him. As I scrambled to my feet, one broke off and came at me but seeing the Colt automatic in my hand, he ran without a word, leaving his fellow attacker. Holmes had placed the other in a choke hold and whispered something in his ear. The man nodded and when released, ran after his companion.

"Watson, you're bleeding. Come, we'll get you cleaned up at home."

Mrs McGuffey was all attention and concern when we arrived and asked for hot water and some towels. She insisted on cleaning me up and, not wanting to go to the hospital, I allowed her to put a few stitches in my head while she thoroughly chastised two "old men" for running about the countryside doing dangerous things, "God knows what!"

"And, Mr Altamont," she continued, "there's a man in the kitchen who's been waiting for you half the afternoon."

"Mrs McGuffey," chimed Holmes, "bring him here, please."

Mrs McGuffey gave him a foul look. "Everything in its own time, Mr Altamont. We take care of the Doctor first."

"Yes, yes, he's taken care of. Now, the gentleman in the kitchen, please," and he shooed her out. "Are you all right, Watson?"

"I'll live. I suppose it was our friends from the motor car?"

"No, two others of "the six" as you call them. I suppose they thought to just put us hors de combat and so solve their problem."

There was a knock on the door and it opened. In walked a man of medium height and build who was dressed as a tradesman and holding his bowler.

"I was hoping you'd get back soon, Mr Altamont." He stopped speaking when he saw me and quickly looked at Holmes.

"It's all right Cusack, he's with us. What have you got?"

Cusack seemed to relax a little and went on. "It's as you said, sir. We've been told to parade Easter at seven at night but the word is it's not just a manoeuvre, it's the real thing. Our lieutenant say's we'd best make Easter duties as some of us won't be coming back. Word came to Cork today."

I could see the excitement in Holmes's face though I'm sure Cusack could not.

"Do you have anything in writing, man? Did they give you anything?"

"Well, no, sir," our informant looked slightly downcast. "Wasn't I right to come to let you know?"

"Of course, man, of course." Holmes reached in a pocket and took out two five pound notes. "Here's for your travel. You've been wondrously helpful."

"No, sir," said Cusack, "I really couldn't. It's for Mr MacNeill after all. I'll fight if they come for us, but just going out and starting it, well, I'm not for that."

"Mr MacNeill would want you to take it Cusack. Here, if anything changes, send me news."

Cusack reluctantly took the notes and departed.

Holmes turned to me as soon as the door shut. "Thomas, are you up to a walk?"

"Certainly, Liam, where to?"

"We're off to see if Hobson is still at work."

Hobson was indeed still at Volunteer Headquarters. We had been in his office but a moment when Captain O'Connell and another burst through the door.

"Just a minute," Hobson said to O'Connell. "What can I do for you, Mr Altamont?"

Holmes reflected a moment, looked at O'Connell and decided to proceed. "Mr Hobson, you guys need to know that I've been told that the Volunteers down Cork way are saying these manoeuvres ain't manoeuvres at all. It's to be a regular American Revolution this weekend and what I want to know is, what's goin' on! I don't mind a fight but let's have the deal!"

It was O'Connell that spoke first. "That's what I've come to tell you Bulmer. O'Duffy here, and I have been told that several of the companies outside Dublin have been told to prepare for an insurrection on Easter Sunday!" O'Duffy nodded and Hobson sat still.

"I've been talking to Managham from Limerick and he had some strange questions about an 'imminent crisis'. I didn't know what he meant."

"Then there's the inconsistencies in the Castle document," chimed in Holmes. "It made no sense from the Brit's point of view. And because of the manoeuvres, the whole Volunteer force will be in arms. Can ya think of a better time or place for a revolt? Can you?"

Hobson sat back in his chair. "So it is to be a rising! They've been planning it all along. Come on then, the bunch of you. We've got to see MacNeill."

O'Connell had a motor car and we piled in and headed for MacNeill's.

Hobson was the first to the door and started knocking as we tumbled out of the car. It was now getting close to midnight.

MacNeill himself opened the door in a dressing gown and pyjamas. "Quiet, please, Gentlemen. Come in to the study. Now what can it possibly be that brings you here so late? More on the Castle document?"

Holmes let Hobson take the lead. Hobson laid out the information he had received from us and O'Connell. He reiterated his fears about the Castle document and the close ties between Connolly, Clarke and Pearse. MacNeill listened intently. "Sir," he finally said, "we've been betrayed! These manoeuvres are just a way to cover for an open rebellion!"

"Pearse would never do such a thing," MacNeill paused, "or would he? It's that old Fenian Clarke! He must have convinced the boy that this is the way. O'Connell, that your car? Yes, of course. Let me get dressed, I'll be with you in a moment then I want you to take me to Pearse."

Chapter 10

Good Friday

21 APRIL 1916

We drove quickly to Pearse's home and knocked. His sister answered the door. She said Padraig was asleep but we heard him call out to his sister that it was all right, he was awake. He waved us all toward the side room.

No sooner were we in the room then MacNeill started. "I want to know what the meaning is of your orders to the companies! Have you told them to attack police barracks and railroads?"

"We had no choice. You had to be deceived. You never would have agreed to the rising."

"This is insanity," stormed MacNeill. "You send men to their deaths like this was one of Connolly's plays on a stage! We can't hope to win. Do you think England will not act? Do you not understand they will bring their soldiers home from the front and stop this? You have no weapons or ammunition worth speaking of, and most of all, the men in the countryside are not trained to use arms even if they had them. How can you do this to our men? Have you no soul? No conscience?" He paused but no answer came. "And what of our word that the actions of the Volunteers would be open for all to see? Yet you do this in secret!"

Pearse was silent, lost in some thought of his own with

half a smile on his face.

MacNeill's rage was spent. He now spoke quietly. "And worst of all, you, a man I trusted, deceived and lied to me."

"The rising will happen, with you or without you Professor. The orders have been sent and the IRB will see that the Volunteers respond. Hobson here is held by his oath." Pearse looked to Hobson.

"No," said Hobson, "our call is for force if Ireland is ready and it is not."

"No, Hobson, they will rise and if we fail, it will not be like you to want of trying."

Pearse looked at Holmes. "Altamont, was not the American Revolution started as a rag-tag type of fight?"

"Mister Pearse, they did it in the light of day with a declaration and a trained militia, what they turned into an Army. Do you intend to do the same?"

"Yes, my friend, I do. I know that we are outnumbered, lack arms and training but we must strike now. It may be our only opportunity. Even if we fail, we will have won."

"The country will not be with you," went on MacNeill. "There are nearly 150,000 Irishmen in uniform. Will their families be with you? All you want is a blood sacrifice."

"It will be enough to make a change."

"No, Pearse, I won't let it happen. You'll not sacrifice boys and old men in a senseless fight they can't win. I'll do everything I can to stop you, short of calling Dublin Castle."

I'll do that, I thought to myself.

MacNeill rushed out of the room and straight through the front door. We hustled to catch up. "I want all manoeuvres for this weekend cancelled, now, tonight!"

O'Connell volunteered to head to Cork as soon as he dropped off MacNeill at his home. When we arrived, Holmes held back as the other three entered.

"It's over, Holmes. Cancelled, or it will be in a few hours."

"No, Watson. I seriously doubt that. Pearse may have to write off the countryside but he and Connolly may still have the power in Dublin to rise here. And we still don't know where or when the weapons are to be landed. Pearse will have to talk to Connolly and the others. We must know what they're planning next."

O'Connell came back out of the house. "Liam, can you find Cacy and send him to Volunteer Headquarters?"

"You bet, mister. I'll go right now."

"Tell him to report to Hobson immediately. You come along too."

"Can't do that, boss. Have to be at the Castle at eight or they might start askin' questions. Doctor here, too. I've got that telegraph to listen to."

"Yes, you're right of course. Well I'm off to Cork." He

disappeared down the street in his motor car.

"What now, Liam?" I asked.

"We send Cacy to volunteer headquarters. Then you head to Mrs McGuffey's. Get a few hours sleep, then stop by to see Hobson at Headquarters before going to work. I'll see you at the Castle sharp at half nine. Room 6."

"But Holmes, what about you?"

"I have other things to do at the moment. Remember, Thomas," he said, walking off. "Half nine, sharp." He nearly trotted into the darkness while I returned home to attempt some sleep.

As it turned out, sleep was almost impossible. My mind would not be quiet. There was to be a rising, now there wasn't. There might still be a rising, but there might not. I had met good men, men who all wanted the same thing, an independent Ireland. Some only by peaceful means, some who said 700 years under England was enough and violence must come. I had always been for Home Rule but were the Irish ever to have it? And what of the Irish who didn't want Home Rule? I felt for Sir Matthew. No matter what he did, he would have the enmity of thousands.

I finally gave up the hope of sleep about six and rang Mrs McGuffey (for somehow the name seemed to fit her better.) for hot water and coffee. Within a half hour, I was walking to Dawson Street to see if Holmes was there. As I walked in, I could feel a great heat and going back to Hobson's office, I found the man busily going through files and throwing papers into a blazing stove.

I knocked and when Hobson turned around he looked startled, then relieved. "Doctor, you're just in time. Give me a hand here. I'm afraid our friends have made a great muck of things." He turned back to the file cabinet. "Grab those papers on the table and throw them in the stove, will you? Good man."

Almost without thinking I complied. The door to the stove was open and I started feeding the fire. Others were coming in now and as each arrived, Hobson told them, "I expect the Brits will raid us. Go through your files and desks. Burn everything that they might use against us or our friends."

I took up a position as stoker. Men would pile papers upon the table and I would feed the fire. It was impossible to discern all that was being consumed by the flames. At nine, I was about to make my excuses and leave when MacDiarmada came in with a note from MacNeill. He gave it to Hobson, who read it once, looked at MacDiarmada and then read it out loud. "Take no action till I see you. Am coming in. MacNeill"

Hobson looked at MacDiarmada. "Keep burning boys," he said and turned back to his file.

I left and walked to the Castle. Constable Flood said good morning and I made straight for Room 6. Holmes was already there. Price, Nathan and Burns followed in quickly before I could speak to Holmes.

"Mr Altamont," started Nathan, as he sat down "DS Burns has been filling me in on your discussions of last night, but I'd like to hear the news from you."

Holmes explained what had happened: MacNeill's cancelling of manoeuvres and his fear that Pearse was still able to do something. "You must move against the leaders tonight," he finished.

"Do we have any proof to use in a court beyond what you and Doctor Ryan have heard?" asked Price.

"No," said Holmes.

"And you won't," I added. "Volunteer headquarters has been burning documents since before dawn." I then added what I had overheard and what Mac Neill had written to Hobson.

"See that!" Burns added. He was smiling but seemed angry. I could not figure the man out. "MacNeill has sent word to cancel the manoeuvres and told his men in Dublin to do nothing. I think any danger there might have been is past. And with Pearse's reputation and good standing in the community, you'll never convict him in a court for doing nothing." He sat there with that artificial smile that made me despise him.

"If," said Price, "there is still to be a rising as Mr Altamont says, we must look at where they would strike, especially with a reduced force. Should I prepare an order to move men from Curragh to Dublin?"

Nathan sat quietly for a moment. "No, Major. I'm not prepared to do that. It might precipitate exactly what we are trying to avoid. The Shinners would claim we were about to attack them and the fight would be on. As long as we hold the railroads, we can move them quick enough. Anything else?"

Holmes was frustrated. "Sir Matthew, if you don't act quickly, you will have a rising, at least in Dublin. When it happens, it won't be just the Volunteers. The ICA, Fianna Eireann, Cumann na mBan, the Foresters and the Hibernian Rifles will all gather. It won't be an event you'll want to deal with, I assure you."

Nathan looked at Holmes somewhat uncomfortably. He finally rose and said, "Yes, well thank you gentlemen. Oh, Price, any word on the arms boat?"

"No, Sir."

"Right, well, good day Gentlemen." The three of them trooped out.

I told Holmes that I had to get to the wards. He nodded and I left him alone sitting by the table.

It was just six when I saw Holmes again at the gate.

"Come, Watson. We have some decisions to make." We walked north toward the bridge. "Hobson has been kidnapped."

"What?" I cried.

"Yes. My people say that Hobson was visited by Neal Daly and Sean Tobin about two and the three left in a motor car. Hobson did not seem to be a willing participant. That can only mean that Pearse and his men intend to continue with or without MacNeill. Pearse has also sent orders for the four city battalions to parade on Sunday at 4."

"What has MacNeill done?"

"They've convinced him to fall in with their plans. They've surely told him about the arms and Casement coming with men.

"What do we do now?"

"I've men out trying to find Hobson, Whether Nathan wants to face this or not, this is far from over. Just before I went off shift I took a message about a man taken prisoner near Tralee who might be a German spy. I think they'll find it's Casement coming here for the rising. We'll have to wait and see. Now, Thomas, a pint and we'll be off to Liberty Hall to see what we can find."

As I had suspected, Holmes' favourite pub was also where he received messages. His contacts had, so far, been unable to find where Hobson was taken but word was he was to be held unharmed. No word had yet come as to who the prisoners were from the sea, for now there was more than one, but worst of all, word of countermanding orders had been sent to the countryside.

"So in less than 24 hours the rising is on, it's cancelled, and it's on. At least that should confuse them all," said Holmes.

"And make them wonder if their leadership knows what they're doing." I added. "Do we go back to the Castle?"

"No, I think not, Thomas. I think we let things play out for now. If it was Sir Roger who was taken, then surely the Navy can take the arms also." He raised his glass to finish it but stopped with it at his lips. "Or so we shall hope!"

Though we stayed till nigh on midnight at Liberty Hall, all was quiet and we departed.

Chapter 11

Holy Saturday

22 April 1916

By Saturday morning even I was confused. I had no idea who was really in charge of the Volunteers or whether there would be a rising or not. The secret society, the IRB, had infiltrated everywhere. But did they control things? Would the Volunteers follow MacNeill or Pearse? The ICA would follow Connolly and the IRB would follow Clarke no matter the consequence. But in all truth, their numbers were inconsequential. Who, I wondered, really held power?

I met Holmes at breakfast and we walked together to the Castle. He already knew the prisoner from Tralee had been transferred to an Army escort and was about to depart for London. We were not to have an opportunity to question him.

A little after 10 o'clock, I was called again to Room 6. I had already tired of what I saw as endless meetings with no resolution. I was not to be disappointed.

Sir Matthew was in a splendid mood for a change and he informed us of the fate of the German arms shipment. The Navy had not only intercepted the shipment of some 25,000 rifles and a number of machine guns, it was at the bottom of the sea. The German crew had, with capture imminent, scuttled the ship in Queenstown Harbour. They had tried to, at least, block the harbour channel but had only been partially successful.

The rebel weapons were gone, at least one of their spies captured. How could there possibly be a rising? Holmes informed them of Hobson's kidnapping and his belief that the rising would still occur.

"I talked with Lord Wimbourne a few moments ago," said Nathan. "He is still insisting on immediate raids on Fr. Matthew Park and Liberty Hall, and arrest of all leaders. I believe, however, that we'd best wait." He looked around the table, smiling with his thumbs in his waistcoat pockets. "I want proof that links the leaders to the arms and spies. We think there are two others still on the loose. Mr Burns, you will work directly with Major Price on putting the information I require together."

Burns nodded. "No danger of a rising now. Even Clarke knows a rising without arms can't succeed."

Holmes rose from the table shaking his head. "Sir Matthew, defeating the Crown forces was never possible. Pearse, Clarke, Connolly, they all have always known that. They see the rising itself as a victory. They are ready to be martyrs to the cause. Unless you do as Lord Wimbourne advises and do it with overwhelming force, I fear you will regret it. Come Thomas, we have things to do." He turned and I scrambled to follow him.

I closed the door and hustled after Holmes, "Surely," I said, grabbing his arm, "with the weapons gone and their spies on the run, even Pearse will call this off."

"No, Watson." He stopped and looked back down the

corridor to the closed door. "Now, they'll surely rise. MacNeill may yet be convinced but the rest will believe that with the guns gone, the Crown will feel more confident and come for them and their arms. And MacNeill has always pledged a fight if that happens."

"Then there is no hope?"

"Wimbourne is not a complete fool. Not as big a one as Nathan and Birrell. I'm afraid, old friend," he patted my shoulder, "the Shinners will have great need of you."

I left Holmes and went back to the wards. The only hope left was if Holmes could somehow intervene for it was certain that Nathan would not act.

Leaving the Castle that evening, I noticed that there were few soldiers about and asked Flood on the way out where everyone was.

"All leaves and passes were approved for the weekend, sir," he smiled back. "Won't be much of anyone around till Tuesday. Monday's a bank holiday and the big races. Most everyone likes a bit o' holiday."

I thanked him, wished him Happy Easter and started to the pub where I assumed Holmes would be gathering information.

I had not entered when Holmes came out the door, turned me around and we headed toward MacNeill's residence.

"It was worse than they thought, Thomas. It is Casement who was caught! The arms, as you know, are gone; one of

Casement's companions is also caught and singing like a bird; arrests of Volunteers have occurred in Tralee and the men who were sent to steal precious wireless equipment to aid the rising are drowned in the river."

"My Lord!"

"Yes, and as for us, the critical time for action is passing. Soldiers have been released for the holiday and Nathan has convinced Wimbourne they should not act.

"And why are we headed to MacNeill's?"

"To see if we can one more time get Mac Neill to cancel the manoeuvres. Perhaps we can at least minimize the damage."

We walked in silence until we reached MacNeill's. We had just rung the doorbell when a motor car pulled up and out got the O'Rahilly, Sean Fitzgibbon and a third man. The door was opened and we all entered.

MacNeill took us into the study, where Holmes told him about all that he had already explained to me. The O'Rahilly explained how Pearse had kidnapped Hobson, and Fitzgibbon told how Pearse had always made it appear that MacNeill was behind all the orders.

MacNeill was horrified; no arms, men dead already, Castle documents bogus. His whole life's work was crumbling in front of his eyes.

"Can we stop it?" He looked around the room.

"We must," said Holmes.

The O'Rahilly was confident. A message to all the Volunteers in Ireland, an open statement to the world from MacNeill that he and his had nothing to do with the arms, and a declaration that he believed the Castle document bogus. It had to be tried.

MacNeill sighed. "To waste lives in a war that is unwinnable is the height of insanity. Worse, it is immoral. Pearse seeks his blood sacrifice."

We waited quietly while MacNeill sat a moment lost in thought. "We must call off this insanity." He turned back to the O'Rahilly. "Take me to St. Enda's school. I must see Pearse. Liam, gather some men who can travel tonight. Meet us at O'Kelly's in Rathgar at nine o'clock." With that they left and Holmes and I started walking toward Volunteer headquarters.

"We've less than twenty four hours to stop this, but it seems that MacNeill has finally settled on a course of action." I ventured.

Holmes was paying no attention to my words. He was watching a man up ahead crossing the street. I followed his gaze and realized it was Dowdle.

"Watson, go to the headquarters, gather three or four men and meet MacNeill, I'm going to follow Dowdle. I'll meet you later."

"But Holmes, you may…"

"Not now Watson. Your duty is the men. I'll find out Dowdle's purpose."

"He's just reporting to Burns," I said to myself out loud, for Holmes was quickly half a block away.

By the time I gathered men and we trolleyed to Rathgar it was close to nine o'clock.

When we reached the doctor's house, the study was already full of men. Many I recognized. Arthur Griffith, founder of Sinn Fein was there, as were other men who were not volunteers. There were also our earlier friends of the evening, plus Joe Plunkett (whom we now believed had printed the bogus Castle document) and Thomas MacDonagh (both IRB men of the first water).

As I was admitted, MacNeill was summing up the situation to all in the room. He was visibly emotional about all that had happened in his name. Griffith stood and looked around the room. He was appalled by what was happening. It was a war of "self-destruction". The argument went back and forth but it was only MacDonagh and Plunkett for the rising, the other eight or ten against. Finally MacNeill raised a hand in the air and slowly fell silent.

"Gentlemen, we shall have no useless slaughter. I am cancelling tomorrow's manoeuvres."

MacDonagh and Plunkett rose together and left the room with the sombre warning that the rising would still happen and those present had added to the slaughter. MacNeill let them go.

MacNeill took out pen and paper and wrote a moment. "How's this?" he cleared his voice, "Volunteers completely deceived. All orders for Sunday cancelled." He looked around

110

and heads nodded. "Where's Liam?"

"He'll be here presently," I said. "I've men here to carry the messages."

"Ah, thank you, Doctor. I'm going to add a note for the Major Commanders. Let's see, how's this? 'Every influence should be used immediately and throughout the day to secure the faithful execution of this order, as any failure to obey may result in a very grave catastrophe.'"

Copies were made and messengers left, but still I knew this was far from over. I left in search of a trolley and Holmes. Not finding him at headquarters, I moved on to Liberty Hall. The place was a beehive of activity. Though near midnight, the place was filled with men in a holiday mood. Here, at least, there was no confusion. James Connolly was in charge and what he said, went! Guards were on the doors as usual and lights blazed throughout the building. Connolly himself was not to be seen nor was Holmes. I finally decided to head for Mrs McGuffey's and some sleep. As I left the building, Holmes was approaching.

"Ah, Thomas, I had hoped to find you. Come, I think it best we get a few hours' sleep."

We started the walk north to Talbot Street. As we walked I related the events at Dr O'Kelly's then asked Holmes what he had learned.

"Dowdle met his cronies and Burns at that warehouse we saw them at a few days ago. I'm sure he was just reporting back what little he knew. However, once their meeting ended, they went out to the four corners of the city. Since some are Volunteers, I wondered what their roles and they moved with a purpose."

"And the purpose?" I prompted.

"Ah, well, to stir up support for the rising. Talk it up, so to speak."

"But the rank and file hasn't been told," I protested.

"True, but if you build discontent, when it is announced, you will have support."

"I don't understand. What has Burns to gain? Some plan of promotion, some sort of revenge?"

"You hold all the clues, Watson. It would not be fair for me to just give you the answer. Besides, I have no proof that Burns could not talk his way out of. It will all come in time. But for now, I believe, some sleep will do us well. Tomorrow may be busy."

As we entered Mrs McGuffey's, events unknown to us were developing. Mr MacNeill would be more resourceful and intuitive than we or his opponents ever dreamed he would be.

Chapter 12

Easter Sunday

23 APRIL 1916

It was Easter morning and as I looked out on the street, I could see the early churchgoers on their way. I was tempted to join them but knew today would be a turning point and I had best await developments.

"Watson, look here!" Holmes had been looking at the morning paper as he drank his coffee. Throwing the paper down on the table, he stabbed his finger at an advertisement.

"Owing to the very critical position, all orders given to the Irish Volunteers for tomorrow, Easter Sunday, are hereby rescinded, and no parades, marches or other movements of the Irish Volunteers will take place. Each individual Volunteer will obey this order strictly in every particular."

It was signed, Eoin MacNeill, Chief of Staff.

"He has certainly bearded the lion in his den." I remarked, pushing the paper back. "Or the Clarke in the tobacco shop." I chuckled at my own sense of humour.

"I believe," said Holmes, "that we have somewhat underestimated friend MacNeill. So have the IRB."

"Surely, it's done then."

"No, Watson. I understand you think me a pessimist but I think this, in the end, will only embolden our opponents.

Pearse will only see it as another betrayal of the Irish cause. He will press on to become a martyr." He stopped to relight his pipe. "And we must not let them have martyrs.

"It's sad in a way, Watson." He went back to the window and looked out. "I truly feel for their cause. Were it up to me, the island would be a dominion like Canada or Australia." He shook his head. "Politicians and power."

"Should we try to see what effect this has had?" I tapped the paper.

"Yes, let's go to Liberty Hall. That's where the nest will be."

By eight o'clock we were entering the Hall, Sean greeted us. "Something is astir," he whispered in his best conspiratorial tone. "Big meeting in Connolly's office." He started naming those who had come through the door: Clarke, Pearse, Mac Diarmada, Ceannt, Connolly and MacDonagh. Plunkett was to be ushered in as soon as he came.

"It's what they call the Military Council," Holmes whispered to me.

"Sean, what's with all the police? There must be twenty of them all around the place," said Holmes.

I looked over my shoulder up and down the street and of a certainty I saw police half a block down on both sides.

A giant grin spread over Sean's face. "It's glorious it is. Two hundred and fifty pounds of gelignite the boys got this morning. Stole it from the quarry. Brought it here they did and

114

those peelers know it. But don't you worry, I won't let them in." He picked his rifle up in both hands.

"Quite a haul, Sean." Holmes returned the grin and patted him on the shoulder as we passed on in. "We'd best see if the bosses need anything. Come on, Thomas."

As we entered, I tugged his arm. "Liam, with that much gelignite they could destroy two or three of the railroad bridges needed to bring the troops in or drop bridges across the river."

"I understand, but that isn't all the explosives they have. I wonder if they got the detonators."

"Liam, Liam, come here." It was Connolly calling from his office. We went straight over. Connolly pulled us into his office where other members of the Military Council were waiting. "Can you get a message out for us at the Castle? It's very important."

"It's my day off, boss. But I ought to be able to get it done without any problem. What ya got?"

"This message must go to our friends in Philadelphia. They will understand its meaning. I don't expect a reply right away so come back when you can." He handed Holmes an envelope.

"Sure boss, back in a jiff."

We left the office, and as we did Holmes instructed me to stand fast and gather what information I could in his absence.

"This will give me an opportunity to talk to Nathan. I'll be back as soon as I can."

While Holmes was gone, I spent my time listening to every conversation I could and trying to keep mental notes on it all. Holmes later told me of his visit to the Castle. He was able to send the wire without any problem. "A fairly simple coded message which detailed the loss of the arms ship and asking for replacement arms from America. Even Clan na Gael couldn't make that happen."

After sending the wire he was able to meet with Nathan, Price and Burns.

"Burns was beside himself with rage. Of course I knew why, but he had to pretend as to his delight with what was happening. Price, of course, wanted to delay until he could bring in troops to Dublin, and Nathan had convinced himself that nothing is going to happen and we should all just smile and go about our business. Never mind the ICA has hundreds of pounds of explosives and a leader willing to use it! All my arguments are to no avail. They will not act!"

It had been near on noon when Holmes returned to the hall, and I had much to report. Members of the ICA had been reporting in all morning. The atmosphere was more like a county fair than a unit about to do battle.

"Well, since you've been gone we've had three men, whom I'm told are printers, brought in. Captain Partridge told them they're under arrest and took them down to the printing press in the basement. They've been hard at it ever since and it's some kind of proclamation. I haven't been able to get a copy yet but the first few words were in Irish in big black letters. The printers have complained freely about a lack of type and decent paper."

"I imagine the boys are 'under arrest' so if things go badly they can claim they were forced to print the document. It'll be their declaration of independence. We'll soon see."

"They're drilling the ICA men and their little council of war has continued all morning. They called me in and asked me numerous questions about the guard mount at the Castle but I'm not sure they completely believed me. I kept to our story of 120 men. I must say I felt a little foolish."

"Don't worry, Thomas. You can always say that's what you saw yesterday. Today they're letting men off for the holiday."

We continued to wait throughout the early afternoon. At one point Mallin asked me to do a review of their first aid stores. It was a miserable lot. They had few bandages and almost no medicines. Some iodine was about the limit. I was horrified at the lack of planning. No unit could see combat with so little preparation. It was if they had no thought of casualties. I reported back to Mallin my findings of their deplorable preparations. "What would you recommend, Doctor?" he asked.

The moment I opened my mouth, I regretted it. "You need to raid every chemist in a mile for supplies," I blurted.

"Give me a list, Doctor, and we'll see what we can do. We won't take anything unless we have to, and then we'll pay for it."

I sat down and started on as extensive a list as I could,

imagining a force of a thousand men and their needs in combat. Mallin left me to fall in with the rest of the ICA who were readying themselves for a march around Dublin. Connolly evidently was planning a march to check the defences of different points in the city. He would watch the response of the different sites to the appearance of 250 armed men. This would give him a better idea of how to take each site. Actually, it was quite a good idea.

While the soldiers of the ICA were gone, the Military Council had broken up. I continued to refine my list and Holmes made his way to the print room to see what he could learn.

It was not overlong before Holmes was back, having confirmed his original thesis that the document was indeed a declaration of independence, proclaiming an Irish Republic. He had not, however, been able to gain a copy.

"Well, Doctor, it appears your information was accurate." It was Mallin, they were back from their march. "When we passed by the Castle, the gate was closed and the guard called out a dozen rifles."

"I don't make a mistake about such things."

"No, you don't. Have that list? I'll get some men on it." He took the list and departed.

Holmes recommended we depart. It was now late afternoon and he wanted to stop into the pub and check for messages. We had but sat down when one of the men I knew to be a contact stopped by to ask Holmes for a light. As he handed back the matches I could have sworn it was the same box he'd been handed. It was not. Our friend had palmed Holmes's and switched it for one of the same make but containing a small slip of paper.

"It appears Lord Wimbourne won't take Nathan's 'no' for an answer. We've been summoned to the Viceregal Lodge at 10 tonight for more talk." He threw the paper in the fire. "Will they ever stop talking, Thomas?"

We drank for a moment before I ventured to bring up the problem, to me yet unsolved: What was DS Burns up to?

"Ah, Thomas, while you would believe me our friends at the Castle would not. In fact, if I told them my suspicions they would put us on the side-lines and make an end of using us. No, I had best keep my own council."

On returning to Liberty Hall we met quite a sight. The Hall was filled with men. Instructions had been given that all ICA men were to spend the night at the Hall. Connolly was busy with men coming and going and the women were in a joyous mood. In the basement, a few rooms down from the printers, men were busy making bombs - some from gelignite, some from powder - and then stacking them in boxes.

Holmes and I decided to split up to see what we could learn. I was near the front door as the sun was setting and came upon our friend Cacy.

"Out running some errands?" I asked.

"Aye. They had me taking messages to the Volunteers. Seems we're all to parade at twelve noon tomorrow. Though they still haven't said why."

"Never mind, Robert. It'll all be plain enough tomorrow."

"I'm sure it will be, Doctor. But my holiday will still be ruined," with that he went on into the hall. "And me stuck here all night with a bunch of tea-totalers!"

Holmes approached from inside. "Time for our walk, Thomas." Off he went, down the street. It was now well dark and as in most cities the streets were, in most areas, poorly lighted. The moon, I knew, would not be up until well after midnight. So in the deep darkness we headed toward Phoenix Park.

The park was probably the most beautiful in the United Kingdom-- 1750 lush acres, and in the middle of it, the Viceregal Lodge. It was toward there we walked. As we passed through the park gate, all light seemed to disappear into the inky blackness. Holmes touched my elbow and held a finger to his lips. I listened intently, trying not to let my footfalls make noise. There were other footsteps. I felt my muscles tense. Surely they would not try again? Were they that desperate to be rid of us? Holmes guided me off into the grass and behind one of the trees that lined the avenue.

Four men passed us by along the road, but even in the darkness I could recognize them as four of "the six". We waited for them to be swallowed up by the darkness, then, using the meadow instead of the road, continued our trek to the Lodge in silence.

From the direction we had taken, we came upon the rear of the Lodge and so made a long sweep to the right to gain the front.

We were admitted to an extraordinarily large study with a massive table. We were evidently the first to arrive.

"Holmes, some days I think I'm getting a little old to be avoiding ruffians trying to do me harm." I threw myself in a chair.

"Never mind, old friend. I'm sure the two of us could have taken them." He smiled as the far door opened. I had not yet met all the players to our coming tragedy, but surely here were the principals: Lord Wimbourne, Nathan, Burns, Colonel Cowan (who represented General Friend of the Castle Guard), Price, Captain Robertson (of the General Staff) and Chief Commissioner Edgeworth-Johnstone of the DMP. Introductions were made of me and Altamont and the meeting started.

Holmes was first asked about what was going on with the Shinners. He explained we had just come from Liberty Hall and everything we knew including the declaration and the assembly for noon tomorrow.

"Lord Wimbourne, we must move quickly or their rebellion will be upon us," he concluded.

"Rot!" cried Burns. "Their arms are in the ocean, Casement is in gaol in London, and MacNeill has cancelled their parades. Even if Pearse calls for a parade tomorrow, no one will come. And Connolly isn't so stupid as to think 250 ICA men can start a revolution." He slammed his hand on the table, again. This seemed to be his favourite antic.

"Mr Altamont," said Wimbourne, "is right. Seize Liberty Hall tonight. Then round up about 60 or 100 of the Shinner leaders and we'll nip it in the bud."

"The Dublin Battalions have been ordered to assembly," I interjected. "Action must be taken."

"Rot!" cried Burns.

"Gentlemen, please. Sir Matthew." Wimbourne stared at the undersecretary. "Act now, in the dark, without delay. By two in the morning you could be ending this whole farce."

"Your Lordship," replied Sir Matthew, "we should end up the farce. We have no proof yet that will stand up in a court of law. I have not yet received any instructions from Birrell and I will not be the cause of an insurrection, which such a move surely must spark." He leaned back in his chair. "I will not have another incident like Bachelor's Walk. Why we might have Shinners rioting in the streets."

Wimbourne looked to the Chief Commissioner. "And you, Sir?"

The Commissioner had been sitting back, his shoulders slumped and appeared lost in thought. Now he threw off his reverie, and sitting up straight, looked around the table. He looked daggers at Burns.

"Lord Wimbourne is right," he started. Wimbourne grinned.

"How should we proceed?"

The Commissioner cleared his throat and continued.

"Your Lordship, we should surround and occupy Liberty Hall, Volunteer Headquarters, and Father Matthew Park and seize all their weapons. At the same time, we should make arrests of all their leaders, forbid drilling, and start a house by house search for weapons."

"And when should we do this?" Wimbourne was obviously enjoying this unexpected support.

"Tonight. We must start immediately." The Commissioner now looked uncomfortable. All was quiet for a moment. Burns was blood red.

Nathan stared directly at the Commissioner. "Can you do this by 2 a.m.?"

"By two?"

"Yes, Commissioner. It will be light by four-thirty. Sunrise is at five, and we must act in the dark."

The Commissioner sat back. "No, I can't. Especially with an unarmed force."

"Colonel Cowan, what forces have you?"

Cowan took a paper from his pocket. "Seventy-six officers and 1465 other ranks of infantry and 35 officers and 851 other ranks of cavalry. With those men, I have to garrison five barracks, the Castle, the Lodge, of course, your Lordship," nodding to Wimbourne, "the magazine, the Royal Hospital and the bank.

"Those numbers leave few men for a round-up of the size you infer. What if our installations were attacked while we were out marching in the streets?"

"There are about 250 to 300 men assembled right now at Liberty Hall," I put in.

Cowan eyed me a moment, then went on. "If what the gentleman has said is true, and they have the gelignite, we'll need to bring in infantry support from the Curragh and perhaps artillery from Athlone." He took a breath. "And it would have to be done in secret or the Shinners will be out and shooting."

"It can't be kept a secret," said Holmes. "Informers are everywhere. The moment you move, it will be known."

"You have a better idea?"

"Yes. You can end this by arresting eight men. Cut off the head and the body will be confused long enough for you to move up the men you need. Dr Ryan and I will return to Liberty Hall and start trying to find the locations of the leaders, for some will be staying in places other than their homes. If you don't strike now, it will be too late."

Nathan turned to the Commissioner. "Do you still say you can't make this happen?"

"Sir Matthew, you know that the only armed part of the DMP is G-Division of which DS Burns is a part. They are only sixteen men. I must have military support."

"Well, your Lordship, I believe that puts us back where we were. I will not arrest without proof or permission from

Birrell, which I have already asked for. I hope to hear in two or three days. In the meantime, Major Price would you meet me at the Castle tomorrow, say at noon?"

The major nodded.

"And DS Burns? I would like you both to help me construct an arrest list."

"I might be a bit late, Sir Matthew, but I'll be there. I'd scheduled a meeting of my men for noon. Won't take but a moment."

"That's fine, Detective. Is there anything else, Your Lordship? If not, I'll wish you all a good night." We all rose and started to depart. As we left the study, Holmes stopped in front of Burns.

"You really need to employ men with a little greater intelligence, you know. Dowdle and his three friends missed us again."

"I don't know what you mean, Altamont, but I think I've only one more need for them," he paused. "Tomorrow." He smirked and walked off.

"What now, Liam?" I asked.

"For me, Liberty Hall. For you, Mrs McGuffey's. I'll meet you at breakfast."

"But, Liam."

"In the morning, Thomas." He departed into the darkness.

Chapter 13

Easter Monday

24 APRIL 1916

"Come, Watson. Breakfast is ready and I fear today you may not eat much else." Holmes was shaking me from my heavy sleep. It had been near dawn when I had finally been able to close my eyes to the outside world and fallen into a dreamless rest.

The sun shone behind my curtains. It was half six by my watch as I gathered myself together. Holmes was almost finished eating when I finally got to the table and as I sat there was a knock on the door. It was Cacy. He and some others had been given a mission to arouse people and get them to their assembly points by noon.

"I'd offer you some coffee but I'm sure you're in a hurry," I told him

"We've always a moment for a cup of coffee, Doctor. It's my only vice you know."

Holmes and I looked at each other and smirked. I poured a cup and handed it to Cacy. "Have you a bit of something to warm it? No? Well, that's fine, any coffee is good coffee."

"Do you have a particular message for me?" I asked.

"Yes, sir, you're to report to Connolly himself and to bring whatever medicines you have with you. He wants you too," he continued, nodding at Liam.

"How is your work going?" Holmes asked, packing his pipe.

"Not finding too many, I'm not. Between the manoeuvre being called off and all, folks have gone on their holiday." He put his empty cup back on the table. "Thank you, sirs, most welcome and refreshing. I'd best be off to see if I can find more folks for their parade at noon." With that, he waved and left.

"Holmes, he still doesn't know what's going on!"

"No, Watson. I left the Hall just over an hour ago and they still hadn't told the rank and file. Some of them have it figured out but for the most part, they are still ignorant of where their leadership is taking them today."

"What were you doing all night?"

"Mostly watching."

"Oh, who?"

"Burns and his men," he fiddled with his pipe. "Can't seem to get it packed right."

"Really, Holmes, can't you just answer a question?"

"Burns and his six minions were surveying their target and I was surveying them. They were also collecting equipment. Uniforms mostly, some weapons, rope, drills and other tools and taking them to their warehouse."

"What uniforms?"

"Volunteer uniforms."

"Do they intend to infiltrate the Volunteers?"

"Watson, Watson. You still do not see. Well, today all shall become clear. Come on," he rose from the table. "Connolly wants you and you can tell him I reported to work at the Castle as usual but I'll make some excuse of illness and come along presently."

As we left the lodgings, Holmes stopped me for a moment at the door. "Have you your identification papers?"

"Still sewn in my waistcoat."

"And your pistol?"

I patted my pocket.

"Good. Be a good fellow and tell Mrs McGuffey to go this morning and lay in enough provisions for a week. She'll understand what I mean. I'll be at the Hall quick as I can."

Holmes left and I went in search of Mrs McGuffey. She only sighed and nodded and I departed for Liberty Hall. "Doctor, do be careful," she called as the door closed.

When I arrived, the Hall was in a state of organized chaos. I sought out Connolly who smiled but seemed very serious.

"Doctor, good morning. Is that your whole supply?" he pointed to my medical bag.

"Yes, what's happening?"

He grabbed me by both shoulders and now truly smiled.

"We're making a republic, Doctor, and you're part of it.

What do you think of that?"

I put forward my best grin. "Let's have at it, I say!"

"Good man. Many of the women here will be working with you. I've got some carts coming and I need you to supervise the loading of our medical stores."

"Is Dr Lynn not organizing that? After all she is your medical officer. First rate one, too."

"Ah, Doctor, she has other things to do this morning. Kathleen will have her hands full so I need you to supervise for the headquarters."

"Of course. I'll go find the ladies now." I went to find my charges. It seemed I would be needed in a professional capacity. I found the ladies packaging their meagre stores. Some had a fair idea of first aid, and others were nurses or students in training, so I saw some hope.

By now, word had spread generally all through the Hall that today was to be the rebellion. The full strength of the ICA was there, about 250. There was also a large group of Volunteers. Some had travelled from Plunkett's down in Kimmage by loading themselves and their weapons on a trolley and paying the two pence fare.

There really wasn't much for me to do yet. One lady appeared to be well in charge and had the women stacking boxes by the door awaiting transport. I decided I could better use my time by trying to gain information to pass to Holmes when he returned. So I went to Connolly's office.Tthe door stood open and I heard voices so I entered. Half the military council was in the room. A map of Dublin lay on the desk. It was Pearse who noticed me first.

"Good morning, Doctor. Come in, you may have need of this information before the day is through." Clarke looked at me, but did not speak. He was not the open trusting kind like Pearse. Mallin smiled and shook my hand, then turned back to the map. Ned Daly was also present.

Mallin's map was covered in dots from various coloured pencils. The colours were grouped in different areas. Mallin explained that each colour represented an area of responsibility for the four city battalions and the ICA or headquarters.

"Once more," said Clarke, "I want there to be no misunderstanding."

Mallin shrugged and with his pencil pointed out locations and named units.

"ICA and headquarters at the GPO. 1st Battalion under Ned goes from Blackhall Place and takes the Four Courts and the area west of GPO."

"I'll send D Company under Sean Heuston to the Mendicity to keep the Brits busy until we're set up," said Daly. "I told him he only has to give us three hours." Everyone nodded and Mallin continued.

"MacDonagh takes his men to Jacob's Biscuit Factory and covers the southwest. He'll have to slow any troops coming from Portobello Barracks. He's going to take Davy's Pub down by the bridge. He'll also be responsible for sending food supplies from the bakery.

"DeValera and his third battalion will take Boland's Mill. The towers will give him great advantage. He'll also take the rail yard, Westland Row Station and have to find a way to hold Mount Street Bridge. It's the most direct route for troops being landed in Kingstown and marched north.

"Ceannt and the 4th Battalion take the South Dublin Union and will have to hold against any reinforcements from Richmond Barracks. I think that is it."

"And 5th Battalion?" asked Clarke.

"Ashe will have a really tough job. He's basically got the whole north side of the city. And I will take 100 men and hold St. Stephen's Green."

"What of communications?"

"We'll have the GPO of course and Michael King and his men will take over the telephone exchange."

"Do we have any numbers yet on how many men are mustering?"

Pearse answered the question. "Not yet. I'm afraid MacNeill has sorely hurt us but we'll have what we have and no more. Surely once we start, the City and the Countryside will come to us."

It was the pragmatist Clarke who broke the silence that followed Pearse's statement. "We've modified the plan,

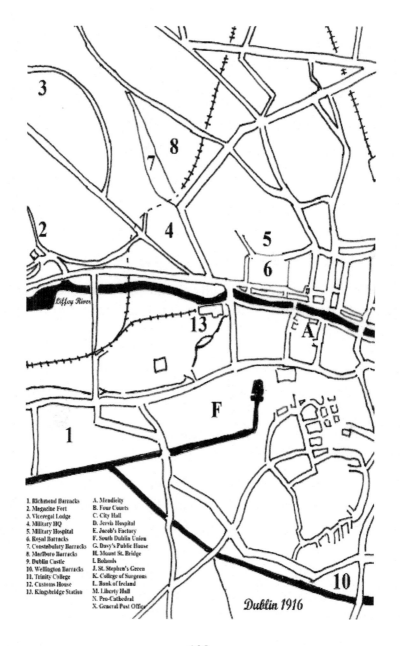

1. Richmond Barracks
2. Magazine Fort
3. Viceregal Lodge
4. Military HQ
5. Military Hospital
6. Royal Barracks
7. Constabulary Barracks
8. Marlboro Barracks
9. Dublin Castle
10. Wellington Barracks
11. Trinity College
12. Customs House
13. Kingsbridge Station

A. Mendicity
B. Four Courts
C. City Hall
D. Jervis Hospital
E. Jacob's Factory
F. South Dublin Union
G. Davy's Public House
H. Mount St. Bridge
I. Bolands
J. St. Stephen's Green
K. College of Surgeons
L. Bank of Ireland
M. Liberty Hall
N. Pro-Cathedral
X. General Post Office

Liffey River

Dublin 1916

132

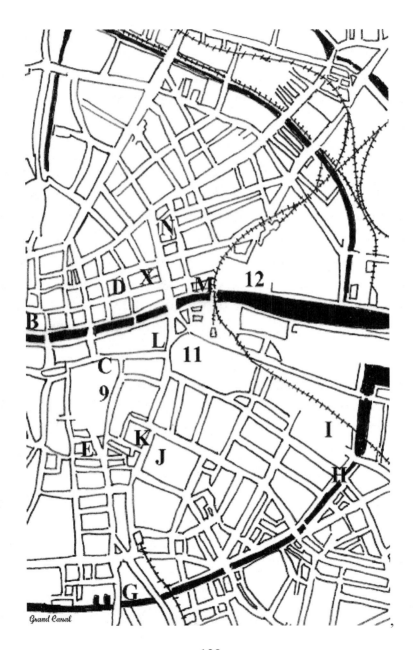

Gravel Canal

we're only taking key buildings and we here all know we can't hope but be defeated in the fight. But we will have risen and we will have done what is right for Ireland. Now, gentleman, let us shake hands and be about the people's business."

As we were about to leave, Cacy came in with a piece of paper, saluted and gave it to Connolly.

"It seems the first numbers are in, gentlemen. 1st Battalion 125 of 350 men are reporting, 2nd Battalion 150 men, 3rd Battalion 130 of 500 and 4th Battalion 130 of 1000. No numbers on 5th Battalion yet."

It was a sombre group that walked out of Connolly's office. Out on the steps, I could hear cheering and quite a commotion. I hustled to the door to find the Countess standing on the steps and reading, in a loud voice, the Proclamation of the Republic. When she finished, she waved the paper about to more cheers. Not only had they declared their independence, they had declared equality for all, both men and women. The cheers continued a moment, then their Lieutenants sent them back to work.

The Countess was ecstatic. She looked quite a sight in her ICA uniform. Breeches, tunic, Boer hat, Sam Browne and pistol. The ICA was the one unit that allowed women in their ranks and the Countess was one of the officers. I had to smile as I thought, "Mrs Hudson would never approve of the trousers, dear lady." But I must say I found the Countess an exciting woman.

It was now eleven o'clock and only 45 minutes before

the Irish Army (such as it was) was to step off. I could not decide if I was watching a comedy or a tragedy. I knew that Nathan would be surprised. Even now while I knew he was meeting with Major Price to start an arrest list, he would be thinking a rising impossible.

The men joked and sang and appeared in high spirits. Their weapons were a motley collection. Most carried the single shot Mauser rifles that had been openly smuggled in at Howth. They were long barrelled affairs that fired an 11mm cartridge (about .45 calibre) and while they could not fire as quickly as a magazine rifle, the large heavy bullet meant substantial damage to anything or anybody who was hit.

There was a smattering of Enfield rifles in .303 calibre with 5-shot magazines, hunting guns, a few American Krag and German Mauser rifles left over from the Boer War, and lots of shotguns. This little Army would find its hands full in a fight. They little knew that Nathan's hesitancy, a liberal Army leave policy for the Holiday, and the need for the Army to protect so many sites, would all work to their benefit. Swift reactions might have crushed them in a day.

As the men were called to fall in a green touring car pulled up at the door. It was the O'Rahilly. He fairly leaped from the car and walked straight to Pearce. There was a moment of tension. Would the O'Rahilly confuse the whole situation? Would he stand on the steps and exhort the men to return home? I could see Pearse hold his breath. But it seemed that even the O'Rahilly felt there was nothing to do now but stand with the men he had trained. He thought the whole affair despicable, but how could he do other than stand with his soldiers? He held his hand out to Pearse. "I've helped wind up the clock. Might as well hear it strike." Pearse took his hand and thanked him. They may not agree but they would stand together.

We were able to load our few supplies in the O'Rahilly's car along with rifles and ammunition and bombs. The men were formed up. Sean Connolly, whom I had seen in the play a week before departed, with a force of fourteen men and nine women. His job was to keep the Castle from reinforcing or being reinforced. The women were well armed with pistols.

Mallin departed a moment later with 100 ICA men to take control of St. Stephen's Green. It was as he was leaving a man came up to Connolly. It was King, the man who was supposed to take over the telephone exchange. This was crucial. Telephones must be cut to keep the barracks from communicating with each other and coordinating an attack plan.

King had his back to me but I could hear him. "Sir, not one of the men detailed to take the exchange had appeared. I must have some others."

Connolly was looking straight at me. He knew I could hear. "Don't worry, Michael," he patted him on the shoulder. "We'll take it later. Right now we have use of everyone at the GPO." King's shoulders sagged as he walked off.

Connolly took a step toward me. "We know there is no hope, Doctor. But it's a start." He turned and walked toward where the columns had formed up.

Holmes had yet to return as our little Army started it's

short march to the General Post Office. For the moment I walked along side of the O'Rahilly's touring car. The best I could estimate was that there were about 150 men and women altogether. Most were ICA, close to 100. The next were Volunteers including the Kimmage men. One tall fellow named Collins walked with Plunkett. Plunkett was recently out of surgery and in his weakened condition should not have even been with us. He would not let his men go without him.

It's but a three minute walk to the GPO from Liberty Hall and waiting for us were Clarke and MacDiarmada. It was just then that Holmes came up to me.

"We're in it now," he said.

"Nothing from Nathan?"

"No. He and Price would only work on the arrest lis., Burns has not appeared so Nathan sent for Norway, who is in charge of the Post Office to come help."

"Charge!" The cry rang out from Connolly at the head of the column. With a rush, the men broke ranks and ran through the doors of the GPO from Sackville and Henry Streets.

"I'm back to the Castle, Thomas," Holmes whispered, and flew down the road as fast as he could run.

The crowd in the Post Office at first took the whole melee as a joke. That is until Connolly fired a round from his pistol into the ceiling. Patrons and workers alike poured out the doors.

"Doctor," said Connolly. "Find a good place for your

137

dispensary. Probably somewhere in the back."

There was a commotion in the centre of the Post Office. Collins had two men at gunpoint, one a constable, the other an Army Lieutenant. The constable stood quietly, hands in the air. The Lieutenant was going on about his status in life and his thoughts about the Volunteers. When Collins felt he'd listened to enough he grabbed down some telephone wire, tied the fellow up and dumped him in a telephone booth, closing the door. Even the constable laughed.

"Where would you like the equipment, Doctor?" It was one of the nurses. I hadn't yet learned names.

I spent the next bit of time deciding on the Postmen's Sorting Room at the far back of the building. It had windows for light and water in two small closets and a passage out to Prince's Street.

Having organized the nurses and given instructions, I went back to the Public Office. Men were busy all around converting the building into a fortress. Windows were smashed now to avoid injury later and then barricaded with whatever was at hand. The building had only been opened to the public six weeks before after a renovation that had taken years. Now the non-supporting walls were being smashed down to make new passages and arms and bombs were being stacked in the general sorting room.

Upstairs there were shots. It took me fully a minute to find a set of stairs and make my way to the floor above. Seven or eight soldiers were under close guard and their sergeant wounded. Up here was the main telegraph office, something the rebels surely wanted to control.

"Let me see the Sergeant," I insisted, and pushed my way through. It was a head wound, not bad, but in need of stitches.

"Is there a hospital close by?"

"Yes, Doctor, Jervis Street Hospital. Just a minute's walk," replied a Volunteer.

"Sergeant, you need stitches and it would best be done there." I turned back to the Volunteer leader. "I'm sending him."

"Of course, Doctor. We'll take the rest downstairs."

"I'm no goin'" cried the Sergeant. "I'll no leave my men nor quit my post until 1800 as ordered."

"Sergeant, you go get treated and we'll let you come back to your post," remarked the Volunteer.

The men shook hands and the Sergeant and his men were escorted out.

I asked the Volunteer as we descended the stairs why there hadn't been more casualties, both sides at close quarters and heavily armed. He stopped on the stairs and turning to me grinned. "They had rifles but no ammunition! Lucky for us, eh?" The squad leader was Michael Staines and I found him to be a fine man.

Back in the Public Office I caught sight of Holmes coming into the building. Spying me, he motioned for me to

139

come outside. I joined him by the columns.

"I was too late, Watson. They had already attacked the Castle and one of the constables has been killed. The gates were closed when I got there."

"Not Flood?" I asked.

"No, another man named O'Brien."

"Still, surely he was unarmed."

"Yes, but the soldiers had weapons. He must have been killed while closing the gate."

Men were passing us as they came out of the GPO and, once on Sackville Street, started running toward the Liffey. I knew they meant to take up positions by O'Connell Bridge. They would use Kelly's Pub and Hopkins on the other corner. Men were now in the Imperial Hotel across the street and a cheer went up as they raised the Starry Plough, (the flag of the ICA), over the hotel. There was a responding cheer and the men in the Imperial were pointing at the GPO. Holmes and I walked out into the street and, looking up, saw the Countess's green flag and the tricolour of the Republic flying where the Union Jack had been.

"What now?" I asked. "We've failed miserably."

"No, Watson, we didn't fail. They would not listen." He reached in his pocket and pulled out his pipe. "Now we at least try to stop Burns. Something good must happen."

"But you still haven't told me what it is. You are really frustrating Holmes!"

"All will be clear by tonight, old fellow." He stopped to light his pipe. "Now, shall we see where the great rebellion stands?" We walked back into the GPO.

As men worked feverishly, Pearce, Connolly and Clarke were gathered together by the counter. Collins was with them, as was Cacy.

"Plunkett has sent someone to the Archbishop?" It was Clarke asking.

"Yes," said Collins. "He wants to be sure the Archbishop is informed. He still thinks we should have kept him informed."

"No word from the battalions yet?"

"Too early, they'll be just getting into position. We do have more men reporting in. Word is getting about already."

"What have we left out?" asked Pearse. "We've sent men everywhere we can reasonably expect to hold, I think."

Holmes took the pipe from his mouth. "Give me a dozen men and I can hold the South side of the O'Connell Bridge."

Connolly thought for a moment. "No. Liam, I appreciate the offer, but we haven't enough men to hold Trinity College and that would be the place to hold. Now come, Padraig. It's time you read our proclamation to the world." They walked off, out of the GPO, and toward where Pearse would announce the Irish Republic.

"Look here, Liam! What's this about a dozen men?" I asked.

He slowly took his tobacco pouch out to recharge his pipe and, while Pearse declared the Republic, Holmes explained. "What buildings are around the Castle? You've walked the city, describe what's there."

"Let's see, Ship Street Barracks, the Daily Express Office, City Hall of course, a hospital, the Telephone Exchange. Trinity College is a block east."

"And across the street from Trinity?" He threw his spent match down.

"The Bank of Ireland!"

"Exactly, old fellow. And it is the bank that is the object of Mr Burns' desire."

"Of course, the uniforms, the weapons. He intends to rob the bank and blame it on the Shinners. But why haven't the Volunteers taken the bank?"

"Well, first off, they know that it's a depository of the People's money and they don't really want to do more harm than necessary. Secondly, the bank is of no strategic value."

"But it covers the bridge and looks into Trinity and it has historical significance. The Irish Parliament met there before it was dissolved."

"Yes, but it has no windows and does have thick walls. You can't shoot from it."

"No windows?"

"It was built when windows and fireplaces had special

taxes. It has no windows to avoid the tax."

I thought for a moment. "But we must stop Burns. How?"

"We shall solve that problem. He won't strike before dark and sunset is not until half seven. In the meantime, we best get back and help the rebellion."

The initial chaos and adrenalin rush of the charge had faded and now men moved with calm and purpose. I decided to check on Plunkett. He had found a stool in one of the offices and sat quietly by a counter, Collins stood with him. He acquiesced to my insistence on checking him. He was fatigued already. I recommended he take himself to the Imperial Hotel across the street and lie down, but he would have none of it.

Hearing constant banging I asked Collins what was going on. "Tunnelling, Doctor. We'll be knocking holes in all the walls that connect with another building. It will allow us to move up and down the streets from inside and not expose our men to travelling openly on the streets where they can be shot."

"A wise device."

"We'll soon be able to move from here to Jervis Street hospital, or down to the river and back, with little exposure - except when we have to cross an intervening road. At those we'll have barricades to help."

I looked about. "Have you seen the O'Rahilly?"

"He's been given charge of the upper floors. The boys will have a tough job."

I could feel movement at my back. Men were running to the doors and windows, rifles at the ready.

"Lancers in the street!" cried someone. I rushed to the doors with the rest. "Keep back, they're forming up at the top of the street," came another voice. All was excitement. I decided to go to the second floor. Where was Holmes? In moments we would be in a shooting war. I found a window from where I could see toward the top of the street.

Lancers in bright uniforms mounted on fine thoroughbreds were formed into line two deep all across Sackville Street. They actually carried lances! This wasn't pig-sticking in India! These men I was with were armed. Antiquated weapons surely but they could kill. "You fools!" I wanted to scream.

Word was being passed around the floor. "No shooting until men and horses are in front of the GPO, per Connolly." Somehow I had to stop this. Taking my pistol from my pocket, I waited. If I could fire a shot just when they were in good rifle range, it might be enough to warn them to fall back. I could claim I was over-anxious.

Now they were moving, lances and polished leather shining in the sun. Damn fools. Closer and closer they got. I held my breath, pointing my pistol in the air, I got ready to fire. They were close now. I must fire now or they were lost. But there was an explosion! The lancers hesitated, general firing commenced from roof tops and windows. The Lancers fell back, up the street and out of range. They left dead men and dying horses but not near what could have happened. I ran as fast as I

144

could go, back down the stairs. I must get to the wounded.

"Hold on, Doctor." It was Holmes. "Those men are dead. But we've a couple wounded of our own. Cut by glass coming in the windows."

I went to our little dispensary where I started treating some bad cuts. One man had shot himself in the belly with his own weapon by accident. I grabbed two able looking fellows and had them carry the fellow to the hospital. As yet, the streets were still fairly safe. That was not to last long.

I went back to the Public Office, searching for Holmes. There I found him with Connolly, Plunkett and Pearse. I could tell we had more men in the building than two hours ago. Plans were being revised. Messengers, mostly boys and girls, were coming and going with reports and instructions.

It was a bit after two and the map that Mallin had left had more markings. Holmes motioned for me to accompany him outside. "Let me bring you up to date, Doctor." He was using me to clarify his own thoughts. "We had our little fight, and we've lots of boys raiding the food stocks and chemists about for supplies."

"It was fortunate someone's bomb went off early," I said.

"Perhaps the poor fellow was handed one with a fuse cut too short?" Holmes whispered to me. "At any rate, there is already general fighting. Some telephone lines were cut but without taking the exchange, they have left communications intact for the Army.

"Sean Heuston has the Mendicity[8] and shot the Army up pretty badly trying to come down the quays. The men at Jacob's Biscuit weren't able to hold Davy's and the bridge, but have stopped any men from Portobello barracks for the moment. The Castle is not taken and soldiers are already arriving in Dublin from the Curragh at Kingsbridge Station. Trinity College is held by the students and some soldiers who were in the area. They've closed the gates and can fire on the Volunteers all the way to the GPO. No real word from Boland's Mill but Mallin is digging in at St. Stephen's and the Countess has stayed to help him. Oh, and MacBride has evidently fallen in with us. Good man to have in a fight."

"MacBride who led the Irish Brigade for the Boers?" I asked.

"The same," replied Holmes.

I made a few excuses about getting back to the dispensary and Holmes tagged along behind with some questions about a blister.

I talked lowly to Holmes as we walked.

"Holmes, this is insanity! They have a score of little Maiwands[9]. These rebels can't hope but to be defeated. Where is the honour in this?"

"It's not the honour, it's the martyrdom, my friend."

---

[8] A stone building across the river and slightly East from the entrance to the Royal Barracks.
[9] Maiwand was the disastrous battle where Watson was wounded in the Second Afghan War. See *Watson's Afghan Adventure*.

"Liam!" It was Collins calling. We re-entered the GPO. "Connolly wants you to try and take a message to Ceannt at the South Dublin Union."

"Come, Doctor, let's talk to Mr Connolly."

Connolly was back at the counter. "Never mind, Liam. I've sent Seamus. The City Hall wants more men, now Sean tells me that Heuston is already surrounded by machine guns at the Mendicity. I've no help to send." He walked to the windows. "And now we've the poor to contend with."

I followed his gaze. Crowds were gathering in the street and already the first stores had been broken into. "They've nothing and now a chance to have everything," he went on, "or so they think." He shook his head. "Excuse me. I'll have to see what I can do to stop this." He walked off.

Sean MacLoughlain was about to bolt out the door and return to Mendicity when Holmes grabbed his arm.

"Hey, Sean, buddy. I need you to do somethin' for me, would ja?"

"If I can, Liam, but I've got to get back."

"Tonight 'bout seven-thirty, I need you to do a job. Go by the main building of the Bank of Ireland. I want to know who's there. Then come tell me."

"Why?" asked Sean with a serious scowl.

"Because I think some rats are gonna take advantage of this and try to break in. We have to stop 'em. Get it?"

147

"We wouldn't do that!"

"Not us! Some rats!"

Sean looked doubtful. "Well okay, but it'll be on the way back here. I've got my duty too."

"Sure, you betcha. But I'm relyin' on ya!"

"Alright," replied Sean, and he was gone.

"Holmes," I whispered. "Shouldn't you get to the Castle and see what you can do to help?"

"No, Watson. This is a military affair now, and besides, no one will want to see the people who can say 'I told you so'."

"No, I guess not."

"But we should be able to get you out of here."

"You jest! I can't leave. We've already got wounded and injured. I must stay."

Holmes just smiled. "I'd best see if I can help with the looters. I'll be back."

I returned to our little dispensary. We were still able to get to the Jervis Street hospital so I evacuated all I could.

It had finally gotten dark, close on to eight o'clock. Runners were still making regular reports. The Mendicity and Jacob's Mill had evidently had the most of the fighting. The raid on the ammunition magazine at Phoenix Park had been terribly botched. Four Courts had seen some fighting with Lancers. The Castle had been reinforced as had the Viceregal Lodge and soldiers were pouring into Dublin from the Curragh and

Athlone. Athlone meant artillery!

Here, tunnelling was still going on. Soon men would be able to travel under cover from the GPO to the Liffey and out the back all the way down the block west. Soldiers were on top of Trinity College and able to snipe the GPO. It was a long shot with iron sights, but random bullets would hit a mark. I would later learn that these were Australian and New Zealand soldiers who had merely been on leave in Ireland and came to the College's aid. Despite the threat of death by the new Republic, looting continued unabated. Pearse might threaten, but he had no heart for shooting the poor.

I had agreed to meet Holmes in the Public Office just after eight and found him there in conference with MacLoughlain.

"Ah, Thomas. Good. We've got to find Pearse and Connolly. I'll fill you in on what the lad has told me when we find them. I think they're with Plunkett in the Bag Room."

As Holmes had said, the three along with Collins were in the bag room conferring.

"Gentlemen," said Holmes, not waiting to be recognized, "you need to hear what this boy just told me."

"Well," said Connolly, looking to Sean.

"Ah, Liam here asked me to check on the bank on me way back next time, so I did."

All looked at Liam but said nothing.

"Well," the boy went on. "I did and we've taken it."

"What do you mean, we've taken it? We don't have anybody there!" shot Connolly.

"There were two men by the door with Volunteer uniforms. There were having to hide pretty good because of the soldiers at Trinity but they were ours."

"What can this mean?" said Pearse.

"It means someone is trying to take advantage of the rising for their own gain, sir. And they'll blame us," replied Holmes. "Give me six men and we'll put an end to this."

Connolly looked at Pearse for a moment. "All right. But I want your man Collins to go also, Joe. The men know him better."

"Of course. Michael, pick five good men. If the bank has been taken by our men, order them out."

"Yes, sir," replied Collins. His dower disposition seemed to disappear. He was a man of action and being constrained as he was in this building was trying on him.

"Doctor," continued Holmes. "I'm most afraid we'll need you also."

"Of course," I replied.

We took our leave of the leaders and Collins went to gather up his men.

"Tell me, Sean," Holmes asked the boy, "can you lead us a good route?"

"Sure, I can. We can still get across Ha'penny Bridge

with no problem, then it's the alleys to the west side of the Bank."

With Collins and his men, we started to work our way through the streets toward the river. We left the looters behind. The streets were deserted and dark. DeValera had turned off the electricity to the trams early in the day, but now all the electricity was off. Keeping low, we hustled across the bridge and past the turnstiles. The British had not yet moved down the Quays but were assembling in Trinity College. We passed down turnstile alley, the dark and the height of the buildings in front protecting us from the view of snipers on the roof of the college.

There was a stillness to our west, to the east came the sound of an Army in motion as men and equipment poured into Trinity. The British were also making use of the early hours of darkness. Only a few hundred yards away men were moving down the roads between the Castle and the College, men who fortunately did not know the area and chose not to leave the main roadways.

We were headed for the west side of the building. Formerly it had been the Irish Parliament (dissolved by the Act of Union in 1801) and now the Bank of Ireland. Holmes already knew where the vault was located on the west side of the Bank. As we neared the bank, we kept to the east side of the alley, moving slowly. Holmes was a few steps in front of me with Sean. Behind me came Collins himself. As we reached the northwest corner of the building, Holmes stopped and motioned everyone to get down and wait. Slowly, he and Sean disappeared into the darkness. We waited there, listening to the noise of soldiers preparing for the next day's fight. It seemed we waited forever but in truth it could not have been more than a few moments. A figure came toward me, slowly out of the darkness. I gripped my pistol until I was sure it was Holmes returning. He whispered for the men to close up and listen to his instructions.

"Sean is watching their one man, who is in the shadow on the far end of the west portico. You can see the glow of his cigarette. He's in a Volunteer uniform, but in the dark it's hard to tell between British and Volunteer.

"Collins, the doctor and I are going to take him. Don't worry how, but when you hear the scuffle, come on. Send two men down the street below. They'll have to make sure no one comes up. Leave one man here and send one to the alley going west. No shooting unless you have to, got it? If you're attacked, hold as long as you can, then make a run for the bridge. You and your other men follow me and the doc here in once we've got their guy on the outside. All you mugs understand? Good. C'mon doc." He stood up straight and walked to the middle of the alley. "Count to 20 then follow us."

Grabbing my shoulder, Holmes started stumbling and singing in a moderate voice. He laughed in a booming voice between choruses of a song I had never heard and half dragged me forward toward the bank. We passed Sean hidden in the recess of a doorway. I could see him grin as I and my drunken friend went by.

Holmes stumbled and sang and as we came abreast of the portico, I saw the glow of a cigarette being flicked to the ground.

"I want me money, Thomas," cried Holmes, in a voice to wake the dead. "These beggars have me money and I need it. What say we go ask, eh?" And we stumbled toward the entrance. A figure in uniform and holding an Enfield rifle stepped out of the darkness.

"Hold up there," said the figure. "Get the hell out with you. The bank is closed and if you don't leave I'll have you arrested." I recognized one of "the six".

"But they have me money!"

"Off with you, I said," hissed the guard. And as he did, took one step too close. With that cat-like reflex Holmes had always possessed, he struck a tremendous blow to the man's jaw, laying him out on the steps, his rifle falling with a clatter.

With a rush, Collins and his partner were there. Our guard was trussed, gagged and dragged into the shadow. At the same time, I could sense the other four take their places and Sean came hurrying up. He gathered up the guard's rifle and melted back into the shadows across the alley.

By now Holmes was at the door listening to find if we'd been given away. He quietly opened the door and we followed him inside. In front was a counter which we followed around to the right. The darkness was horrible. Moonrise would not be until two in the morning, so even with the large door behind us open there was only blackness.

As we came around the corner I could see a dull light

from under a door. In here, there would be no danger of someone outside seeing it and investigating. Holmes stood, charged the door, and burst in. The guard here must have been standing with his back to the door, for he was thrown onto four other men who were lying, bound on the floor in front of him. Before our victim could recover, he found Holmes on his chest and a pistol in his face. A candle glowed on a small table. We had the second of our six in hand and tied up with four British soldiers on the floor. Holmes instructed Collins' man to stand guard on our prisoner, then he, Collins and I went on down a corridor to a large double door. I knew we must be outnumbered now. Surely Burns and Dowdle were here with their other three minions. As we slid through the double doors, Holmes whispered to me, "Remember, it's Burns we want. The rest we can always have."

We moved along a second corridor to a stairwell. I could barely see at all when Holmes flicked on an electric torch. "Someday I must thank Mr Hubert for his invention," whispered Holmes. We moved down the stairs, all three pistols in hand. The vault would be below.

We exited the stairway and Holmes switched off the torch. Down the hall, to the right, we could see the glow of lamps and hear men working. We tip-toed down the corridor and, almost as one, the three of us gazed around the doorway. Inside the room were six men. Burns was chastising his thugs to hurry and fill Army kit bags with money while Dowdle held a gun on the man I imagined who had been "persuaded" to open the vault.

"That's it boys," said Burns. "That's all us rebels can carry," he laughed, as the men picked up the bags.

"And him?" asked Dowdle, pointing at the banker with his pistol.

"Why, he died trying to save the bank's money."

Dowdle smirked and cocked the hammer. I didn't wait. I stepped into the light, my own pistol pointed at Dowdle.

"I do not believe that would be advisable Mr Dowdle," I said. "Now put that weapon down."

For an instant, everything stopped. There was no movement anywhere. Dowdle must have thought me alone, for he merely smiled.

"Why, sure it is, doctor," he replied. But I had learned long ago to watch a man's hands, not listen to his words. Instead of dropping the pistol, he pivoted toward me, weapon level. His shot went wide, mine struck home, followed by another. Afghanistan and South Africa had both taught me to make sure my foe was down and not able to make a second effort.

Holmes and Collins were now in the room. Burns and his three friends all had their hands in the air. The banker still stood in terror, his back against the vault wall. I went to Dowdle, but he was already gone. "It didn't have to end like this," I said, to no one in particular.

"Never mind, Doctor. " It was Holmes. "Let's get these others out of here."

"Sir," he addressed the banker, "we are going to remove

these men. Would you be kind enough to re-close the vault door?"

The banker nodded. I could tell he was in shock but for now, at least, he could function.

"Collins, if you'll go first, these four gentlemen will follow. Doctor, grab the lantern. I'll come along with Mr....?"

"Brooks." Stammered the banker.

"First, let's get this man out of your vault. Grab a hand there, that's it. Now shut the door please and lock it. I'm sure you can put all that money back on the shelves later."

I had moved into the hallway with the lantern and it was here I made my mistake. Collins was moving slowly in front, then Burns' three men, then Burns. All had their hands in the air. I walked up behind Burns, pistol in one hand, lantern in the other. I knew I was too close when, with one motion, he turned to his left and caught me in the face with his left hand. I went sprawling, still clutching both pistol and lantern.

A rifle is a fine weapon but not in a close space. As all four made a run at Collins, it was more use as a club than a firearm. He was thrown to the floor in the rush and the gun went off. Another man down and Burns and the other two were sprinting up the stairs three steps at a time. Holmes passed before I or Collins could get off the floor. Collins followed Holmes as I looked to Burns' man. He was dead, the bullet having entered the chin and gone through the top of his head. Brooks was beside me in near panic. Holding the lantern and pistol in one hand, I took his arm and guided him up the stairs.

At the room where we had left all the prisoners, I found Sean, Collins, the men we had left, and Burns' companions who had followed him up the stairs.

"Where's Liam?" I asked.

"Gone after some gent," replied Sean. "They moved too fast for me, but I got these two trying to come out," he gestured with his newly acquired rifle.

"Which way did they go?"

"Over toward direction of the Castle."

I pondered for a moment. What was I to do? It was pointless and dangerous to go after the two of them. I didn't know where they would run. And the soldiers were likely to shoot any civilian in the dark.

"Doctor," said Collins. "We'd best do something with these men."

"Sean, untie the soldiers."

"What?"

"Untie the soldiers. Tie up this lot." I pointed to Burns' men. "First stack all the rifles over here by me. Now just tie their hands behind their backs. Collins, re-call your men. We'll be taking these imposters with us."

Collins had his men gathered in moments.

"Mr Brooks, I put these four soldiers of the King in your care. You will not be molested again. I assure you these men were bandits and no part of the Volunteers. I think that once we are gone, these men will be able to re-arm themselves over at Trinity College."

Seeing that we had all the arms and our four prisoners, I asked Sean to lead us back. We moved swiftly back across Half Penny Bridge and north to the GPO.

As we entered, I could see a line of men waiting to say their confessions to Father Flanagan, but I had more need of some rest. Wherever Holmes was, his battle with Burns was now his. It was just now half ten and Collins took charge of our prisoners. I could hear firing in the distance. The firing would go on all night. It was left to me to explain our adventure.

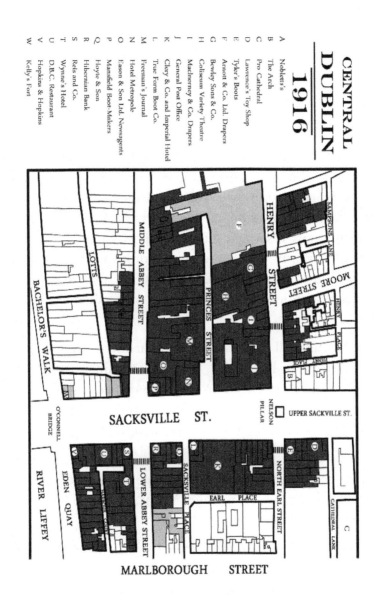

159

Chapter 14

Tuesday

25 April 1916

It had taken past midnight to explain to Pearse, Connolly and the rest what had happened. I thought it best not to tell all I knew. I explained how we had found the seven men trying to rob the bank and had stopped them, how we had turned the bank over to the now disarmed guard and how Liam had gone after their leader. Burns' men were quite morose without their leader and kept quiet. At least they understood that to admit their complicity with a G-man would only make their plight all the worse.

I could tell that Collins thought there was more to the story than what he knew, but said nothing and asked no questions. I went to check on my little dispensary. Considering our meagre supplies, the ladies had done admirably with our few patients who had not been evacuated to the hospital.

By one in the morning, I had found a nook and fallen to sleep. I knew I could not impact whatever Holmes was doing, and somehow I now felt my age. Many's the time I had slept to the sound of gunfire.

It was just past three when I was awakened. "Thomas, time to get up old fellow. We've places to go." It was Holmes. I wiped the sleep from my eyes and looked at his face in the candle light. Even now, I marvel at his energy.

"I see you wasted no sleep on worrying about me," he grinned.

"Fairly pointless, old fellow. I'd no idea where you went, but I had faith in you."

Holmes laughed and sat back on a pile of mail sacks.

"And Burns?" I asked.

Holmes face did not lose its smile. "Dead, I'm afraid."

"Did you?"

"No, not me, old friend." He reached in his pocket and retrieved his pipe. "Soldiers of His Majesty's Army meted out the punishment."

"But how?"

"Oh, they thought he was a rebel I suppose. I chased him west toward the Castle, then up to the Quays and back east and finally south toward College Street. I suppose he was trying to make it to the police station." He stopped and lighted his pipe.

"And?" I prodded.

"Well," he drew in some smoke. "I suppose the soldiers in Trinity College took him for a rebel. I mean, in the dark, civilian clothes, running down the street. Pretty valid assumption at most times. Once he went down, I watched some soldiers go to him. They left him there on the street. No point in bringing in a dead man."

He leaned back further into the sacks and closing his eyes, puffed slowly on the pipe.

"So without knowing it, they have served out the King's justice," I mused.

"Quite, and we, my friend, should be off." He stood up and looked at where I sat. "Dawn comes at five, it's near four now and it'll be lightening in the east. Our mission is done and we need what little darkness is left to get to the Castle and not end up like friend Burns."

I stood for a moment and looked at the dispensary. The ladies had formed themselves into shifts and, while some slept, others tended the wounded.

"No, Holmes, I can't go." I looked at Holmes, who only nodded.

"I thought you might say that."

"I know warfare, Holmes. This is going to be very bloody. All they have is a few nurses and a medical student. Good lad by the name of Jim Ryan."

I paused, thinking. "I can't say I'm not in sympathy with their cause. The country has been treated shabbily. I just don't approve of their method. But I can't leave men who I know need what little skill I possess. Can you understand, Holmes?"

Holmes put a hand on my shoulder. "It's what I expected, Watson. Exactly what I expected. But I had to come and give you a chance to get out. By tomorrow, the men north and south of the Liffey will be cut off from each other."

"I appreciate it, Holmes. But my duty now is with the wounded. I'll be careful and I still have my papers." I patted my waistcoat.

We shook hands and Holmes turned to go. "How will you get there?"

"Oh, for now, across Capel St. Bridge, then through the alleys to the Castle. I'll have no problem."

"And what will you tell them about Burns?"

"That I haven't decided. Well, Watson, be careful." With a quick wave, he was gone. I went out into the Public Office. Things here were quiet for the moment. Plunkett was asleep on a cot that had been brought out for him. If anyone had no business being out in this mess, it was he. He should have been convalescing at home from his surgery.

It was now near dawn and the streets were dangerous again. The snipers at Trinity College could drop rifle bullets all around us. I could hear a roar of gunfire down by the river and to the southwest just a bit. The Army must be attacking city hall. They needed to drive the rebels out so they could have free movement in the Castle yard and civil government have a place to work. The thought kept coming back, "a score of little Maiwands". I suppose our American cousins would call it "little Alamos". I shook my head. Had the war in France taught these men nothing? A static defence against overwhelming power? To me it made no sense. And soon we on one side of the river would be cut off from those on the other side. Their very plan had meant disaster. Had all the men been between the Liffey and the Grand Canal, how much better for command and control it would have been. Or between Liffey and the Royal Canal, at

163

least then they could escape into the mountains. But it was not my job to fix their deficient plan.

Dawn had come. It was about five in the morning and the firing was dying out from near City Hall when I heard the rattle of machine guns. I approached Collins and asked what he knew.

"Not much, Doctor, I do say I don't like being in this box for the Brits to shoot at."

"Nor I. Any word from outlying points?"

"Our people are moving quite freely still. I fear the City Hall has probably fallen, but we've other men in the buildings in the area. Worst is that Mallin is catching hell. Brits have put machine guns in the Shelbourne Hotel and are cutting him up pretty badly."

Connolly walked up to us and asked Collins to check on the tunnelling efforts. The tunnel from the GPO to the west had just started. But work should be progressing from the Liffey.

"I'm sending men over to the Metropole Hotel, Doctor, and we'll be putting up some barbed wire across the road. With the sniping from Trinity, I expect some casualties."

"I see our looters are out again," I remarked. "You'd think they'd stay in from the bullets."

"What more fear have they of bullets than of everyday life? No, Doctor, they don't fear death. For these people, death is a relief." He looked down and started to walk away when an ICA man stopped him.

164

"Excuse me, sir, but I need to leave for a bit. I've got to get to work."

"You what? This is a war, man!"

"Oh, I understand, sir. But I'm the only one with the keys to the warehouse and me mates will lose a day's pay if I don't open up."

Connolly looked stunned, then looked at me and laughed.

"I understand," he replied, "but once you've opened up, remember we need you here."

"Course, sir, thank you."

The man gave a salute and scurried toward the Henry Street door as he checked his watch.

The morning continued with sporadic fire from Trinity, looters in the streets, tunnelling, and the building of barricades. For me, there was a constant flow of minor injuries, mostly glass cuts, or misdirected shovels and picks.

Our British prisoners were put to work in a make-shift kitchen and actually seemed to be having a good time. The nearby hotel kitchens had been emptied of supplies. There appeared to be adequate food to go around. Burns' men had been taken to the basement and locked in a small room to be dealt with later. There had been sporadic fire in the looted buildings and the fire brigade had been risking both irate looters and occasional bullets trying to put the fires out. So far, they were successful. It was going late morning when Sean O'Kelly brought the first bad news. City Hall and the Express Office had both been taken and British troops had free movement in and out of the Castle. There were but a few Volunteer snipers left in the area.

About noon, a large number of re-enforcements arrived, about 65 in number. They were immediately divided up and put to work. A barricade went up on lower Abbey Street and the tunnel from Sackville Place to Lower Abbey Street was finished. On into mid-afternoon things around the GPO were still fairly quiet.

I could imagine Colonel Cowan's plan, if he was still the senior man present. I speculated that Brigadier-General Lowe would probably be here by now. There was no need to rush. We had bottled ourselves up. Cowan only had to gain strength then take out each strongpoint one at a time. He'd probably concentrate around the Castle first and the Viceregal Lodge. Then St. Stephen's to be sure of a route from the boats for more troops. All he really had to do was make sure we stayed put and ran out of food and ammunition.

It was mid-afternoon when Sean MacLoughlain ran into the GPO. "Doctor, have you seen Mr Connolly? Ah, never mind, there he is."

I walked over to where Connolly stood next to Pearse.

"Sir," went Sean. "I can't get back across the river. We're fairly cut off. Without swimming it in the dark, I'm not sure how to get across."

"Can we still communicate with Ned Daly at the Four

166

Courts?" asked Pearse.

"Yes. sir." He looked at me. "And we've got a hole yet to the hospital, doctor. I knew you would ask." He smiled. This was without a doubt, the bravest 15-year-old I had ever met.

"You've done well," said Connolly. I could tell he truly liked the boy. "Stay close, we may need you to run more messages soon." I went back to my dispensary. There sat Holmes on a pile of sacks.

"Liam, what...?" I asked.

"Couldn't leave you alone, don't know what you might do."

I knew he could have stayed out of danger and yet he came back to help a friend. I didn't know what to say.

"Well, where do you need me?" he continued.

"I do need more supplies, so anything you can go out and find would be appreciated." I moved closer and whispered, "How the devil did you get back?"

"All the way up by the Grand Canal and then south," he whispered back. "Plenty of open ground if you're willing to leave the main roads. They're moving around in an arc all across the north side. If our friends don't decide to get out soon, they will not get out."

"Liam!" It was Connolly, "Where have you been?"

"Out scoutin', boss. Like Sherman through Georgia. Pickin' the place clean for the Doctor here."

167

"Excellent. Listen, I've just heard from Fergus O'Kelly. The wireless is up and running at Reis's. I need this message taken there and sent to the world. Everyone must know that there is now an Irish Republic and that the Republican Army holds Dublin. Come back and tell me when it's sent."

"Right, boss," replied Holmes and started to leave only to be stopped by a rush of men entering the building. It was a dozen or more with four or fiveprisoners.

"Mr Connolly, sir," said one, "we've had to fall back. They're using artillery on us now. Blew up our barricades by north Circular Road Bridge and kept moving south, they did. We picked up these boys along the way." He pointed at the prisoners with his rifle.

Holmes looked at me with a stare that said, "I told you so." Shrugging his shoulders, he turned to the door and was gone.

Connolly had been busy questioning his men about the situation to the north. I recognized one man instantly as an Army doctor, a Captain.

"Captain, I see you're an Army surgeon. How did you come to be here?"

"Home on convalescent leave," he said with the thick accent of County Cork.

I extended my hand, "Doctor Wa....Ryan. I may have need of your help, sir."

"Captain Mahoney," he replied, taking my hand. "I'm a

doctor first and will do what I can."

Connolly had ordered the prisoners to the kitchen, but quickly acceded to my request to leave Captain Mahoney with me.

By seven in the evening, our casualties in the GPO were still minor, more accidents than anything else. Holmes had long returned from the wireless school and ensconced himself in the dispensary as my orderly. It was he who told us Pearse was to speak outside and deliver a message as to the state of the Republic. Leaving Mahoney, Holmes and I went to the street. There I was to hear a man I had respected, Pearse, tell bold-faced lies to the crowd. We were winning, Ireland was rising, Irish regiments of the British Army were refusing to fight. All of this he knew was not true. Truth was not convenient. It was discouraging to hear.

"Who does he think came from the Curragh and Athlone, Russians?" whispered Holmes. We returned to the dispensary.

The rest of the evening I spent going about the upper floors checking on the men. Those on the roof were most exposed and I knew that by morning the British would probably be in a position to make their lives hell.

A runner came in after dark looking for Connolly. He found him in the General Office with Plunkett and Pearse. Holmes and I were listening to their plans for victory. It all seemed hollow. They knew what would happen. But the runner made it worse.

"There's a gun-boat on the Liffey, Mr Connolly." He was a young man of the Fianna Eireann. There was silence a moment.

"They'll be able to place artillery fire directly on Liberty Hall from the river," I exclaimed. I couldn't help myself.

Plunkett looked up from his cot. "He's righ,t you know."

"We've nobody there now but the caretaker," said Connolly. "There's no need to fire at it. Besides, a capitalist army will never fire artillery at shops and businesses in their own city. A few of our barricades to the north here was one thing. But their own city centre? Never!"

Collins was standing nearby and listening. I could see him shake his head and walk off. He was angry. He hated this "box" he was in.

"Let us hope so," said Pearse. "Liam, go above and ask the O'Rahilly to have his men watch carefully for the gun boat."

"Right, boss," he replied and started to move away toward the stairs. "Feel like a walk, Doc?"

"Coming, I need to check on the men again anyway." I followed him.

"Connolly is wrong, you know." Holmes said. They'll burn the city to the ground before they let the rebels have it."

"What do we do?"

"We do what we can to save lives."

"Do you report back to the Castle?"

"Report what, Watson? That nothing's changed and that they are winning? That these men are determined to be your 'little Maiwands?' They already know that. No, we must try and influence things from within here. Ah, there's the O'Rahilly."

Holmes communicated his message and we returned to the floor below. Sixty more men had come in. Connolly was busy dividing them up among the GPO, the Metropole and the Imperial. For a little while I watched the flow of burning buildings and the shadows of the fire brigade as they fought to extinguish the flames. Finally Holmes and I went back to the pile of mail sacks to try to get some sleep.

Chapter 15

Wednesday

26 APR 1916

I made rounds about three in the morning to check all our wounded. At the moment they were fair, so I returned to my mail sacks. Young Ryan and Captain Mahoney would be more than able to handle things. Holmes was awake and smoking another pipe.

"Have you decided how to influence things?" I asked.

"Curious problem, Watson. We cannot be overly strong to stop the fight or we shall be written off as cowards and our words ignored. If we do nothing, things will resolve themselves, as we know they will, with great loss of life. No, we must play the middle path, trying to make them see their foolishness but preserve their pride." He grew quiet for a few moments and I sat back down.

"I believe, Watson, we must make sure they have all the information we can give them and let them come to the final conclusion. They are intelligent men. Soon they have to realize they must save lives. They've made their blood sacrifice. It's time to stop."

"How will you get the information?"

"I intend to go to the Castle or the Royal Barracks, find Nathan, get all the information I can on the troop strengths and disposition, and return here."

"How will you explain how you got all this information?"

"Ah, well, Mr Pearse is going to send me on a reconnaissance mission." Holmes winked at me. "He just doesn't know it yet."

I shook my head. "He'll know it shortly, I'm sure," I muttered.

Holmes got up and brushed himself off. "I'll be back in a bit. I need to talk to Pearse alone."

I pulled my hat back down over my eyes and listened to the occasional rifle fire in the streets and how it echoed. Trying to sleep was useless, so after a few moments I went to the floor above and made my rounds of it and the roof. I could get the first sign that the end was in sight. As I moved among the men in the growing light, one called my attention to the Liffey.

"Look at the city crew," said one of the men pointing across the river. "They're working on the street. The fools are likely to catch it." He shook his head.

We all strained to see in the early light. Sure enough, they were tearing up cobblestones in the roadway across the river. The men talked among themselves and made sure no one would fire upon the work crew. I dared not tell them what it really meant. I decided to find Connolly and explain what was happening. This was the kind of information that was needed to stop the fighting.

I found Connolly and Clarke as usual in the main office.

The increased crack of rifle fire could be heard with the first light. There would be another day of bloodshed.

"Mr Connolly, have you heard that road crews are digging up the street?"

"Yes, Doctor. Life must go on, I suppose. It would be better if they had rifles instead of shovels and picks."

"Then you don't know what it means?" I asked. But I knew he didn't.

"Means?"

"Yes," I looked hard at the two of them. "It means cannon! It means they're bringing up the artillery to shell us into submission!"

The two looked stunned for a moment and then, to my horror, began to laugh.

"Don't you understand?" I asked. "It's time to evacuate, disperse, move to the mountains. To stay here and be destroyed by artillery would be folly."

"Doctor," replied Connolly, "I thank you for your advice, but they will no more fire into the city than they would burn it. The capitalist owners would not stand for it. Believe me, it's one thing to blow a few barricades, but not the city centre. Now, let's hear no more of it."

"But what an honour it would be James," said Clarke. "It would mean they took us seriously."

I now knew that I could never get through to these men.

The cause was all there was. I would have to save those that I could, one at a time. A cry came down from the roof. "Gunboat!" We raced past the upper floors and then to the roof. Indeed, the gunboat that had been reported at the mouth of the Liffey was approaching the Customs House. She was a small ship, a single funnel craft. I was later to learn that her name was *Helga* and that she had been used in patrolling the fisheries before the war. Now she patrolled the coast looking for German submarines. She sported what appeared to be a 12 pounder cannon fore and 6 pounder cannon aft. She had a Holmes searchlight near the bridge for night time use.

She anchored by a Guinness boat but as she was moving up I could see more activity from down near Tara Street. The O'Rahilly was by me at the upper window. I pointed to the men. "Two 18-pounder cannon. I'm afraid Mr Connolly is wrong. The capitalists will shell the city. They've dug up the road so the spade of the pole trails could dig into the dirt. They'll be able to fire in a moment."

The O'Rahilly seemed lost in thought. "I tried to tell them," he said quietly. "But now we must do our best. Hold on long as we can, then perhaps, go to the mountains."

"It looks like they've laid to fire on Liberty Hall."

"Yes. They probably think we'd not give it up without a fight." As if a man shaking off the doldrums, he shivered a bit, smiled and slapped me on the back. "We've a real war now, Doctor. A real war. You'd best get back to your dispensary."

"Time enough for that yet." The occasional crack of

sniper fire was all that was to be heard at the moment. I could see the artillerymen readying their cannons.

The first shot came from the *Helga*. It completely missed Liberty Hall and hit an intervening railroad bridge.

"Too direct a shot," I said to the O'Rahilly. "They'll have to fire under the bridge. Those naval guns shoot too flat a trajectory."

He was as fascinated by the scene as I was. He nodded and continued to stare at the river. Now the two cannons on the street opened up. The 18-pounders roared and bucked, their spades digging into the ground where the cobblestones had been removed. The *Helga* now had the range and was firing more rounds into and around the hall. The *Helga's* sighting was poor and as many shells landed on the buildings around the hall as on the hall itself. The machine guns started playing their tune on the empty hall. The firing came from across the river. There was also rifle fire, but I could not tell from where it came. I decided to go back below and await development.

Captain Mahoney and Jim Ryan were in the dispensary when I entered. Ryan was anxious for news of the shelling, so I sent him to the front of the building.

"I thank you for your help, Captain. This can't be easy for you."

"It's a sad situation, I agree. But if we concentrate on saving lives, that's what's important."

"Doctor!" Ryan rushed in with a wide grin. "Cannons,

machine guns, rifles, and old Peter ran through it all. They never touched him!"

"What are you talking about, Ryan?"

"Old Peter Ennis, the caretaker at the Hall. He answered the door when the *Helga* "knocked" and ran through it all. It's a good sign, Doctor."

I hoped, in my heart, that he was correct. The shelling was like a flame and all the citizens of Dublin moths. Both soldiers of the Republic and citizens of the city were attracted to the sound and fury. They were fascinated by the oncoming destruction, just as I had been, the first time. Everyone rushed to the windows save Mahoney and me.

"I don't suppose our friends have any artillery to respond?"

I had to laugh. "No, Captain. I'm quite sure they don't."

"Well, that's something anyway. Surely it will end quickly now."

"Not if they keep shelling empty buildings," I replied. I was occupying myself checking supplies for the hundredth time; they were still meagre.

"Ole Spence here has been sloppy with his work. Can I get a bit of help here?" Two men had entered, one holding up the shoulder of the other as he hobbled in. Both Mahoney and I went to them.

"What have we got?" I asked.

"We just finished the tunnel up from the Liffey and Spence here puts a pick in his leg with the last swing. What a clown, eh?" He smiled at his companion and we put him up on a sorting table.

"Well," I said, looking at about a four-inch superficial tear in the calf. "That's pretty serious. We'll bind it up and then I want you to take him to the hospital for some stitches. They can do it better there." Mahoney looked at me out of the corner of his eye. "Right you are, sir," continued the companion. "I'll get him there in a jiff."

I tore away Spence's pant leg, used some peroxide and put a bandage on the wound, sending the two on their way. Mahoney came up to me once the men had left.

"Two less rifles?" he whispered.

"Two less dead men." I replied.

Leaving Mahoney in the dispensary, I went back to the General Office. The cannons were still shelling an empty building and the machine guns were still rattling hundreds of rounds into barren windows.

Connolly and Clark couldn't be happier.

"If they're willing to destroy their own shops and businesses, we must be winning, eh Doctor?" cried Connolly.

"No, it's a war, sir. They'll do what they need to do to end it. That's all it means."

"Doctor, the whole world is at war. Why? For Belgium and the right of small nations to exist, at least that is what they

178

say. Had they given Home Rule as promised, I doubt they would be here. There would not have been the need. We'd eventually get complete independence by parts. At least that would have been the general wisdom. But they won't give us peace or our country back. We must fight. We're taxed greater than England itself, our patriots are deported, and they want to draft us into their army to fight for their cause but not our own. At some point we must say 'no'. At some point we must fight. This is that point."

I looked around at the many men in the GPO. "I understand, Mr Connolly."

"These men will fight because it's the right thing to do."

"Excuse me, Mr Connolly." Cacy approached without so much as a sound. He was fumbling with his cap. "I'm supposed to report to you with some information, Sir."

"Yes, spit it out."

"Well, Sir, they're landing at Kingstown. Hundreds of them."

"You see, Doctor! They do fear us. They fear the people will rise with us." He turned back to Cacy who was still fumbling with his cap. "Is there something else?"

"Yes, sir. Mr Heuston, sir. He's surrendered the Mendicity. Low on ammunition and surrounded by machine guns."

"He did much more than was asked, Cacy. He was to hold for three hours. He fought them for three days. He did well.

Now, Cacy, find me Mr Collins. I want him to make sure our tunnelling is proceeding to the west. Do you think you can get through to DeValera?"

"I can try, sir. But I doubt it. I'm willing to try."

"Then do it. He must stop those soldiers from crossing the canal. The longer we hold, the better our position. No, on second thought send Sheehan. He lives in that area and can give an excuse for being there. See him off and come straight back."

"Aye, Sir."

All was quiet at the GPO for the moment. Mahoney and I were discussing the casualties to come. The looters were still on the streets, though there was less and less for them to rummage through. What hadn't been carried off was being set on fire here and there. In fact, around noon, there was a large fire in Henry Street, but the fire brigade dealt with it fairly quickly.

It was early afternoon before the attack came directly toward the GPO. By mid-morning, the Army had stormed Liberty Hall and found no one in attendance. The shelling had temporarily stopped but I could see the 18-pounders being manhandled toward a grassy area south of O'Connell Bridge. If I was right, they'd start by firing directly into Kelly's or Hopkins and start north, one house at a time. But what was happening in other directions? It was Holmes who answered that question for me.

I had been making my rounds to check on those who had been slightly injured. On returning to the general office, I found

Holmes in conference with Pearse and the rest.

"Ah, Doctor, you're just in time. Liam was about to tell us what he's found out. Continue, please." Pearse turned to Holmes.

"It's like this, boss. Ya got lots of soldiers coming into Kingsbridge Station. They're going to the Royal Barracks, then in a big ring around us to the north. The Castle is full of soldiers too. So is Trinity College. Must be thousands there. Your man DeValera has some of his boys by Mount Street Bridge. When I left, they was trying to hold up the whole British Army coming from the boats. Half the soldiers gettin' off the boats is just goin' around them straight to Kilmainham or the Castle. They have a least four cannons, that gunboat, and more machine guns than I've ever seen. All that ammunition in Phoenix Park is still there. Your guys didn't damage a bit of it when they tried to blow it up." Holmes looked around at the assembled leaders. Each stood quietly, thinking his own thoughts for a moment.

"Let me tell ya, gents," he continued, "if you're going to get to the mountains, you'll have to do it before dark 'cause by then they'll have you like rats in a trap. Then all they gotta do is wait. We'll run outta food and ammunition. I might be able to get back south and tell the rest of the boys to just disperse as best they can."

"Not time for that yet," said Connolly. "I hope DeValera gives them hell. We still have direct contact with Ned at the Four Courts." He turned back to Holmes. "What about the rest?"

"Well, Ceannt and MacDonagh are holding on but

181

they're each surrounded. The Mendicity is gone, so is City Hall and Mallin is shut up in the College of Surgeons. No one can move. Bunch of little Alamos, eh Doc?" He winked at me.

"Have you noticed the cannons south of the bridge?" I asked.

"Yes," replied Connolly. "I've ordered our men to fall back through the tunnels when the artillery starts. They've nothing but a rifle and a few shotguns down there. They'll come back to the Metropole."

It was Collins who seemed the most distraught. Here, I thought, was an ally. He wanted to fight, but not here in this box. He wanted to go out and take the fight to his enemy. Maybe we could get him to make the others see the light. Their mission had been accomplished. Ireland had risen. Why waste lives? Fight later on better terms.

"Collins," I ventured. "Could you get these men out of here and to the mountains?"

"No!" cried Clarke. "We stand and fight! Ireland must come to her senses. She will come to her senses. We must show that a just cause will win out!"

I could see that Holmes, Collins, and I would be the only dissenters. The O'Rahilly I thought would be with us but he had put himself in exile on the upper floors. He rarely came down.

The roar of cannon dispersed our little group. So close were the cannon to their targets that the sound of the firing was almost simultaneous with the explosion of the shell. That target was Kelly's at the end of the street on the corner of Bachelor's Walk.

"Cacy!" called Connolly. "Anyone seen... ah, there you are. Across to the Metropole, friend, and make sure our men got out of Kelly's. Let me know, off with you."

"I'm back to the dispensary," I said. Machine guns were now pouring thousands of bullets into what we hoped was an empty building. "Liam, I could use a hand."

Captain Mahoney was waiting for us. I explained to him, Ryan and the ladies what was happening. None seemed concerned and in fact, the ladies seemed elated. They were making the British enemy fight for every street. To them, this was success. I had to admit, from their perspective, in a way, they were winning. They had declared their independence, formed a government and were fighting a fair fight.

The afternoon dragged on with a constant crack-boom from cannon and shell and the buzzing of machine guns. Holmes and I had retired to our mail sacks to discuss our next move. The truth of the hopelessness of the situation seemed to gain us nothing. What were we to do? I had seen this before, both in Afghanistan and in South Africa. It seemed the more hopeless the cause, the more desperate the fight.

For more than two hours the cannon and machine guns played on the empty building. I had decided to go to the roof to peer down the street when someone came up on my shoulder, Collins.

"Are they ever going to attack?"

"Not yet," I replied. "They want to cross the bridge and since they have plenty of ammunition and time is on their side, they'll destroy both sides before they try and cross. At least, that's what I'd do."

"Me, too, Doctor." We knelt behind the statue of Hibernia and watched for a few more moments.

"Ah, look Collins, they're traversing the cannons. They'll start on Hopkins now. Once they're sure the other side of the street is destroyed and abandoned, they'll cross."

"The boys upstairs will have something to say about that."

"What's that?" I asked, hearing a machine gun.

"Another machine gun."

"I know, but it's coming from the west."

I was right. The Army had placed a machine gun on the top of Jervis Hospital and was pouring down fire on the GPO. We rushed below to pass the word, but they already knew.

"Liam! Liam!" I could hear Connolly calling at the top of his voice. "Someone give me a pencil and paper! Find Liam!"

I turned to Collins. "He's in the dispensary." Collins went off to get him.

"Blackguards know we won't shoot at a hospital," railed Connolly. "We'll obey the rules of war, even if they won't."

Holmes came in with Connolly. "Yeah, boss. Whatcha' need?"

Connolly was writing furiously. "Can you get through the hole in the wall into Jervis Street Hospital?"

"Sure, boss."

"Take this message to whoever is firing that machine gun. They know we can't shoot back, but we can do something else. If they don't stop, we'll start shooting prisoners."

"But you can't!" I blurted out.

"Of course not, Doctor. I wouldn't even think of it. But they don't have to know that." He looked back at Holmes. "Do you understand, Liam? You must make them believe it."

"Don't worry, boss. I can do it. Let me get my cap, Doctor, I'll be back."

Holmes was gone for more than an hour. The others worried but I realized he had taken the opportunity to get to the Royal Barracks or the Castle. It hadn't been twenty minutes before the firing had stopped from the roof of the hospital, so we knew he had delivered the message. By the time he was gone 90 minutes, they had decided that his mission had made him a prisoner, so when he appeared after two hours, they were all amazed. The word he brought was both good and bad.

"The boys at the hospital have been hidden by the good sisters," he told Connolly. "The Brits believe them to be regular patients. The bad news, boss, is that they've got armoured cars."

"Really, have they now?" Connolly was joyous. The worse the odds, the better it looked for us if we hold out, was his thought.

"They've mounted steel boilers on some lorries and put gun ports in them. They're using them to cut us off from the Four Courts." He looked at the floor, then back up at Connolly. "We're surrounded, boss. One man might get through at a time, but other than that, we're caught."

"How do you know?"

"I went lookin'. Only reason them cannons haven't blown us sky high is they can't get a clean shot from across the river cause of the buildings." Holmes took another long breath. "Only chance I know might be east, then north, once we cross the rail lines."

"Thank you, Liam. We'll take that into consideration. Doctor, would you and Liam like to get a bite? Tell the kitchen to send some tea if they can. Thank You."

Holmes and I had obviously been dismissed so the council could talk. We went to the makeshift kitchen where I delivered the message and then out to our little sanctuary of mail bags. We sat on the sacks, tea in hand, listening to the cannons destroy the jewellers on the corner opposite Kelly's Pub (another now empty building), while machine guns rattled between cannon rounds.

"Think they'll listen, Holmes?"

"No, Watson, not so long as Connolly and Clarke are running things. Pearse is the weak link here. He's willing to die for the cause but he's a pacifist at heart. He doesn't like to see others injured or killed. He's the one we have to work on. His poetic soul makes him vulnerable. You can see that the minor suffering so far has already caused him pain." He took out his pipe and started to charge it. "Yes, Pearse is the one to get to. Problem will be that the others will cause him to stiffen his backbone. He won't want to appear weak. We have to convince him that they've made their point, it's time to stop." He lighted the pipe and leaned back.

We sat for a few moments, quietly, in our sack-filled closet. I was startled by voices by the door. It was Connolly with his teenage son, Roddy, and an ICA man. Connolly was talking quietly but firmly to the boy.

"You must get through to Bill O'Brien with this message, Roddy. That's why I'm sending the two of you. Once you've delivered it, stay with Bill, he has work for you."

"But, Da," protested the boy. "I'm needed here."

"You're needed with Bill. Those are the orders."

"Yes, sir," replied the boy and turned to go.

Connelly and the other men shook hands and a knowing look passed between them. Then the ICA man turned to follow the boy out the Henry Street door as Connolly walked back to the front.

"Holmes, did you…"

"Yes, Watson. I'm afraid it's a bad sign for us. He sent the boy out of harm's way. He means to stay at all costs." He kept drawing on the pipe. I sat, thinking there was some way to stop things. Nothing came to mind.

Suddenly I realized that the cannons had stopped firing

and even the machine guns were quiet. It was just an occasional popping of rifle fire. I got off the sacks and went to the front of the building. I could see that Hopkins Jewellers was on fire, as was Kelly's, I assumed. I couldn't see Kelly's but there was smoke. I wondered if the 18-pounders were using incendiary shell instead of high explosive. Either could cause a fire but the incendiary was designed to. Of course, I reasoned if they could destroy the buildings that blocked the GPO, they could shell it also. I wondered how all the other "little Maiwands" were doing as I returned to the infirmary. Night was starting to fall and I could feel the first emanations of a fatalistic turn in our little garrison.

With the dark came relative quiet from outside the GPO, but inside was quite different. As I made my rounds that evening the men were together in small groups singing songs. Pearse was philosophizing to a few and Clarke held a group enthralled with stories of the old Fenian days. By the time I had checked patients and seen to the men on the roof, I was feeling tired. I went in search of Holmes. He was gone, so I turned my sacks into a couch and tried to sleep.

Chapter 16

Thursday

27 April 1916

It was just before four o'clock that I awoke to movement. Holmes had returned and was seated across from me, pipe still lit and a sadness on his face that I will never forget.

"What news?" I murmured, not moving.

"They've done exactly what you predicted, Watson, though it hasn't gone all the way of the Crown." He tapped the doddle from his pipe on to the floor. "Each little strong hold has been surrounded. They're not going to pay much attention to any of them, just keep them bottled up. They made a try at the South Dublin Union and got bloodied for it. The worst was down by Mount Street Bridge over the Grand Canal. They marched men up from Kingstown and tried to cross a bridge that they could easily have bypassed." He started to recharge his pipe, his head shook back and forth and he let out a small sigh. "Over 200 dead and wounded in one spot. Of course, they're claiming there was a whole company of rebels, but I doubt there were more than a dozen who cut them up in a nice crossfire."

"What next, Holmes? We're cut off from everywhere. I'd think they'd come after us, then, with the headquarters gone, They'd call for the others to surrender."

"Oh, exactly right. Lowe is still in charge and he's

planning on taking the GPO. Today if he can, but he's willing to wait. Soldiers are pouring in and he has no desire to be accused of wasting lives. By dawn he will have cannons north and south, armoured cars in the streets and the ability to grind us down slowly." He looked at me for a moment and taking the pipe from his lips, looked down at the sacks. "I don't suppose you'll agree to leave now? No, of course not, but I had to ask."

"Do you know what's happened to the Countess?"

"Ah, well, I should have known you'd ask that. She and Mallin are surrounded in the College of Surgeons. They can't move without machine guns tearing the place up. As for the rest, Four Courts is surrounded, as is Jacob's Biscuit Factory, Boland's Mill and the South Dublin Union. They're all ineffective at this point. They can be starved out, if need be. Oh, Lowe will have his men harass them, have no fear. Some cannon and machine gun fire will keep them awake and on their toes. But he'll wait it out until he's taken to the GPO. But now" he stood "let's get some tea and see what we can do to convince our rebel friends to concede."

It was as we took some tea in the kitchen with our prisoner workers that the renewed assault began. By half four it had started in earnest. From the upper floor and the roof, movement could be seen all around us as Lowe closed his forces ever tighter. The machine gun and rifle fire were sporadic but heavier than through the night and seemed to come from everywhere. As yet, there was no cannon fire.

Holmes went to pass all the information he had gathered to Connolly and Clarke. His knowledge was explained by his night reconnaissance. But what should have made them see it was time to stop just made them dig their heels in all the more.

"The longer we hold on, the better our place at the table when the war is over. How can they claim they fought for the rights of Belgium, a small country, and deny us?"

As it would turn out, after the Great War, even the American President Woodrow Wilson would not listen to them at the Paris meeting in 1919.

At six o'clock, another call came down from the roof. The three stacks of the destroyer HMS Dove could be seen drawing into the Customs House. Did it mean more troops or just more cannon? We did not know at the time it was the return of Birrell. His time left in Ireland could be measured in days.

Holmes spent the rest of the morning with the hierarchy while I attended to the infirmary. By mid-morning, the cannon had added in their bark and it was not long before the surrounding buildings were starting to blaze. Now, however, there was no fire brigade. It was far too dangerous for the men to try to put out the flames with machine guns raking the streets. I continued to be amazed at how comparatively few casualties we had.

The coming of the cannon fire brought new machine guns. The bullets came from the Gresham Hotel to the north and Lower Abbey Street to the south. The rebels sniped away, hoping to make them keep their distance. In this they were most successful.

It was shortly after this, while I bandaged another glass

cut, that I heard a cheer from the Public Office. Clarke had sent a young girl (Leslie Price) to the Pro-Cathedral for Father O'Flanagan to hear confessions and take notes to families. Putting on his traditional stove pipe hat so he could be identified as a priest, he and the young girl had dared cannon fire and machine guns crossing Sackville to the north and then down Moore Street and through the tunnel to the GPO. Here were two true acts of bravery. One might fault rebels or the Church in many things, but bravery was not a shortcoming in either. The Archbishop had been irritated at the fact that he had not been advised before the rising of what was to come or asked his permission. But when the British asked him to interfere on their behalf he had sent them off with a flea in their ear. In fact, as I was to find, some of the Church were the biggest supporters of the rebels.

I found Holmes in with Connolly, Plunkett and Pearse. Holmes had been a wealth of information to them. But no matter the darkness of the picture he displayed, they hung to an unreasonable combination of hope and fatalism. Holmes knew he could not demand they listen to his continuing words but he must win them over with the argument of saving lives.

"We've had a few casualties here," Clarke was saying. "Each a tragedy, yes, but some blood is always lost."

"And you've lost quite a few at Mount Street, the Mendicity, and the Union" Holmes said. "Ask the doctor here. He's fought the Indians in Californy when they was hold up. Comes a time to go, eh, Doc?"

"Er, ah, yes, certainly. If there is a way to slip out we

ought to save the people from harm and save their homes from destruction. I'll tell you it's getting very hard to get through to Jervis Street Hospital and we can't do a lot for the wounded here. We have stretcher cases now that should have gone."

I could see we were getting through to Pearse. He was wavering, starting to ask himself at what point do we stop. It was Plunkett's aid Collins who spoke up. "I, for one, believe we should try for the mountains. It's a long time until dark, but we should get out of this trap and keep the fight going in the countryside."

"Sorry to interrupt, sirs." It was our friend Cacy. He looked tired, his eyes sunken from the lack of sleep, and he kept rotating his cap in his hands as had become his nervous habit.

"Yes, Cacy," replied Connolly.

"You Gentlemen need to come see this. They've got lorries what are bulletproof."

"Ah, yes, Mr Altamont had been telling us. Where are they? Show me."

"Right, Sir. One's on Henry Street and the other is by the bridge. Haven't moved this way yet."

We all, save Plunkett who was lying on his mat, started for the front of the building. It was just as we moved that there came the crack of a cannon to the north and the slam of a shell into the Metropole Hotel across the street. It was indeed all too late now. Cannon north and south, armoured cars in the streets and machine guns in all four directions. The lid on the box was

193

closed and we all knew it. It was a stand to the end, a bloody fighting withdrawal or surrender. Those were now the only alternatives.

The machine gun fire increased, but most bullets went high in the windows, hitting the back wall. The cannon, whether north or south, still couldn't get a good angle at us yet. Our own men in the outlying buildings poured fire out as best they could. While the lorry on Henry Street was stopped by one of the rebel barricades, the one on Sackville slowly moved north, bullet after bullet slapping the sides of the boiler turned armoured plate. As dozens of rifles tried to shoot into the gun ports cut in the boiler and meant to shoot out of, the lorry rolled to a stop. It was deluged in a thunderstorm of bullets which seemed to last forever but had not been more than a minute. As suddenly as the storm had started, the firing stopped. What had happened? The iron creature sat still. Had they shot up the motor where it could not run, had the transmission gone out, or had the driver been killed with a lucky shot through the eye slit?

We could not go out to the iron lorry and any soldiers inside dare not come out. The men in the boiler were trapped as surely as we were.

"We've got to improve our barricades," Connolly muttered looking about, he grabbed a half dozen men to follow him out on the Prince Street side. I went back to the infirmary. Holmes came with me. He was as near to exhaustion as I had ever seen him. His inability to impact the situation, I knew, was infuriating to him.

"You can't control everything, Liam. Emotions don't

lend themselves to logical resolution." I could see him breathe deeply and look down at the floor.

"We should be able to control these things. But it's like the greater war, each side will only stop at 'victory' no matter the cost or the logic of it. Look outside, Thomas, the second finest city of the empire is burning. Why? Because, each side sees violence as the only answer."

"Sometimes it is the only answer," I sighed. "Submission is against human nature, and wrongs, or perceived wrongs, cannot be dismissed. Sometimes it has to be washed away in blood. At least, that's how humans feel. In a way, it's a shame the good Lord gave us both reason and emotions. They are so often contradictory."

Holmes was looking directly at me with a quizzical smile. "There are times you astound me, Watson." He walked toward the Henry Street door and gazed out. "I'm off to the Castle. I can have the most impact there."

It was odd how the rattle of machine guns had become just noise. It was the crack of the 18-pounders that brought me out of thought and back to reality.

"How Holmes? We're surrounded. Wait until dark at least."

"I'm certain I can get through the tunnel, over the rooftops then through the hole to Jervis Street Hospital. They're not firing from there anymore."

"Holmes, please, just this once listen to me. Wait for

darkness."

"Dr Ryan! Dr Ryan!" Cacy was racing toward me. "Mr Connolly has been hit, come quickly!" Connolly was walking calmly behind him, as if nothing was wrong, but holding his left arm wet with blood.

"In the infirmary, sir. We'll soon take care of you." Turning back to where Holmes had stood I saw nothing but empty doorway. Holmes was probably halfway to Jervis by now. I followed Connolly and Cacy into the infirmary, still shaking my head.

The wound was not at all critical. It was more blood than damage. Our medical student, Ryan, did an admirable job cleaning and tending it. There was little for me to do but watch. Our nursing staff swarmed the poor man. It was no wonder he wanted to get back to the fight and away from the attention. This he did as quickly as possible. In the space of twenty minutes he was thanking everyone and, putting his jacket back on, went to the Public Office. I decided to once again make a round of the upper floors, but first made a tour of the ground level.

Our numbers had swelled since we first came to the GPO. It was hard to estimate how many we had now. Men were tunnelling through walls half a block away, they were barricading at a frantic pace on the ground floor. (Clarke was as positive that there would be a final bayonet charge by the British as I was sure that there would not be.) I was certain that Lowe had learned something from the Great War, and that would be "don't waste soldier's lives in foolish charges against even antique firearms." There were more men in the surrounding buildings, especially at the Metropole and the Imperial Hotel, the other two strong points. But volunteers were spread from Lower Abbey to Cathedral Lane and Henry Street to Middle Abbey. Men and women bustled all about me.

Leaving the frenzy below, I went to the upper floor. Here there was more of a calm. I was greeted with the usual good humour of the men. Except for some complaints of not being relieved and going for long periods without food, all seemed in good spirits. Every minute or so came the crack of a rifle from a southwest corner window. I went over to a young volunteer kneeling at the sill.

"What are you shooting at?"

"Oh, that tin can on wheels there, Doctor. Every now and then I pot at it. Just to remind them that we're out here." He smiled up at me chuckled, "And they aren't!" He turned back to the window and fired off another round. The clang of the bullet hitting the disabled armoured car was clearly heard. I put my hand on the boy's shoulder.

"There are men in there, you know. Men like you and me. I understand the need to keep them where they are, but try not to enjoy it. It could be you someday."

The boy looked at me as if I were some museum oddity, then looked out at his target. Without looking back at me, he replied, "I understand, Doc. Don't worry, I'll just remind them now and then that we're still here."

As I continued my round of the floor, I saw Connolly,

197

and it looked like young MacLoughlain, lead a large group of men onto Princes Street, which was fairly well protected with a barricade on the east side and dead ending into a wall of a building on the west. I watched as they continued south down an alley about mid-block, which led to Middle Abbey Street. I wondered their purpose. Too many men for a reconnaissance. Was it a flanking attack of some sort? In fact, Connolly had taken the men out to work on fortifying a barricade, but I would only learn this later.

Having finished my round of the first floor, I continued to the second. My reception here was much as the floor below. There was a certain tenseness in the air, but the men were still in good humour and looking for the final fight. Here I spent a little time cleaning a few cuts. It was as I finished that I took the time to look out of the south-facing windows. There, on the ground by the alley where Connolly had led his men, I saw an arm stretch out from the side of the intervening building. The hand clawed at a piece of cobblestone and pulled so that the next moment a head appeared from behind the brick. Leaving my vantage point I sprinted down the stairs to the ground floor, across the Postman's Sorting Office that served as our dispensary and out the Princes Street door. The only thought in my mind was that Connolly must be saved. He was the logical leading force. If he were lost all would be chaos, and surely it was his head I had seen appear. As I crossed the infirmary, I called for Ryan to follow, and bolted across the narrow street to the alley. As I knelt next to Connolly, he nearly smiled. "Can you give me a hand, Doctor? I need to get back to headquarters."

"In a moment. Let me take a look here."

Ryan was now with me, as was Captain Mahoney. Connelly had been shot in the ankle and there was no way but to carry him to the infirmary.

Once inside, the poor man was once again surrounded by those wishing to help. I'm afraid I made few friends with my demands that people leave and stay out of this. I had Ryan find Cacy and had him give instructions to keep everyone out until we could deal with the wounds.

Mahoney was a fine doctor. I deferred to him. I placed a tourniquet on the leg while he cleaned the wound and Ryan got the pieces for a splint. The ankle was terribly shattered. We had no morphine for the pain, little antiseptic, and no anaesthetics.

"Ryan, my boy, send anyone you can to the chemists shops they can safely reach. We must have some morphine."

"Yes, Doctor, right away."

"Captain Mahoney, I must admit you're younger and steadier than I. I'll loosen and tighten the tourniquet as required. Would you see if you can extract the loose bone chips?"

"Of course, Doctor."

Connolly must have been in severe pain, but he refused to show it. Many were the men I had treated in Afghanistan and South Africa, but never had I met one who dealt so well with his suffering. Though the tears of pain were in his eyes his smile stayed and he spoke words of encouragement to those around him. Even severely injured it was clear all would turn to him for guidance. The women crowded around him until the press of bodies became such that I had to demand they leave the area. But no matter my words, they would not go. I changed strategy. "Mr Connolly, would you be good enough to remind my helpers here that we have other patriots in the room."

Through his agony, he had the ability to laugh. "Ladies," he announced in a booming voice, "I thank you for your concern but I'm not badly done. Please help the others that are here while the good doctors look to this minor injury of mine. Please, ladies."

With some additional prodding on my part, they dispersed. One lady refused to go and I did not press the issue any further. Ryan's men had worked quickly and some morphine had been found. It wasn't much but it would have to do.

The crash came without warning. Plaster and dust cascaded around us as Mahoney threw his body between the debris and the open wound. As the dust started to settle, Mahoney raised his head to me. "They've re-laid the cannon, Doctor."

"Yes, they've found the range. We're in for it now." I gazed up at the ceiling. "Upper floors and roof I think."

Another artillery round crushed above us. Again we were enveloped in dust. "Mary," I asked of one of the ladies, "get us some hot water from the kitchen and see if we have an umbrella."

"Umbrella?"

"To help keep the ceiling from falling in the wound."

"Oh, of course, Doctor, right away."

"You have some fine people, Mr Connolly." I paused and peered at the man on the sorting tables. "Be sure you remember to take care of them." Mahoney stopped in his work. He and Connolly both regarded me for a moment.

'Doctor," replied Connolly with a slow meaningful nod. "I know what you are trying to say. I know that while you are with us your heart is not in the fight. You think this has been an error. It hasn't been." He looked about him. "Never fear," he sighed. "It'll be over soon." He smiled and placed his head back on the table. "We've won, Doctor. You'll see."

Mahoney shrugged and went back to cleaning the wound.

"I'm afraid we've done all we can, Doctor. He needs to go to the hospital."

"No, I won't go! I stay with my men!" Connolly's look was intent.

"Never thought you'd do anything else, sir" smiled Mahoney, patting Connolly's arm.

"Let's get him off this table and onto a cot, Captain."

We took him out and placed the cot near Plunkett in the main room where he was immediately surrounded by the men, each more concerned than the next. I returned to the infirmary and left them to their task. The ladies were working down the sorting tables as I entered. We now had nearly a score of injured. I needed to triage so that I could get the worst men out to the hospital. Mahoney made no arguments to my decisions as he too knew we had to move men safely. The artillery was coming more frequently now, both here and among the buildings south.

The O'Rahilly came into the infirmary and looked about.

"Any prisoners in here, Doctor?"

"Just Captain Mahoney, but he's more help than prisoner."

"Well, I'm moving them all to the basement for safety. We don't want them injured by their own shells."

"I'm needed here," piped up Mahoney.

"Yes," I affirmed. "He's of great value here."

"All right, but we must protect the rest. The rules of war demand it, and it's only the right thing to do."

I took the O'Rahilly by the elbow and walked to a far corner. "We've been able to put the fires out and no one has been badly hurt so far. But the fires toward the Liffey are out of control. Clery's store and the Imperial Hotel are on fire. Men are coming in the best they can from the outposts. We've no way to fight the fires."

I looked intently at him and he smiled a crooked smile. "I know what you're thinking, Doctor." He straightened his body and lifted his shoulders. In a loud voice hecontinued, "Yes. We're doing quite well. If you see them bring in any more prisoners, send them down, will you Doctor? I'd best be above to my men." He patted my shoulder and walked off to the stairs to the upper floors.

"Ryan," I called. "Make a round of the basement, will you? Mahoney, you stay here. I'll start around."

Men were still working steadily at barricades and re-dividing ammunition amongst themselves.

"They're running for it," shouted a voice from the front. With the call came a deafening roar of machine guns. There must have been a half-dozen guns streaming 600 rounds a minute, pouring up and down Sackville Street. Despite the noise and danger, men rushed to the windows like moths to the flame. Bullets popped the inside walls, but all seemed to be high. The men yelled encouragement as six volunteers made the insane charge across the broad street from the burning Imperial Hotel to the GPO. As each man reached us he was cheered, but then there was a collective moan. The sixth man had gone down in the street and did not move. In the midst of celebration was sadness. It was a horrible let down. I forced my way to the front at the call for a doctor. One man had cut himself badly leaping through the broken windows. The machine guns continued for a few seconds then fell silent. I checked my new patient. Lots of blood and he'd need stitches. I stood up to ask for some help moving him to the back, when, from the corner of my eye, I saw movement. It was from the street. The man we thought dead was up in a moment and running for us. It took the machine gunners by surprise also, for he was fair in the building before they got the first shots off. He was being pounded about the back and shoulders by his comrades and heartily cheered. It was all I could do to force my way to him.

"Are you all right, my boy?"

"Yes, sir. But I learned a valuable lesson." He looked about with a broad grin. "Don't fall down when people are shooting at you!" There was a general laugh and cheer at this. I made my way back to the infirmary.

Mahoney had our latest casualty well in hand so I decided to go above and make my self-imposed rounds.

Above were the signs of fires that had been recently extinguished From the windows I could see a short distance north and south. Across the street, the Imperial Hotel was going up in flames as were most of the buildings on that side down to Upper Abbey Street and on down toward the river. Connolly and Clarke couldn't have been more wrong about the "capitalists".

It was close to dark before I finished. The shelling at the GPO was intermittent and the 18-pounder shells made little impact on the solid outside walls. The flames of the explosions constantly started fires which had to be quickly extinguished. There was now no need for lights on the upper floors for the burning buildings that surrounded us made a glow that must have been seen for a dozen or more miles.

It was fairly quiet in the infirmary. In the Public Office, great activity continued unabated.

Explosions were coming from down the street. Seeing Sean Duffy at the door, I went to find out what was going on.

He stood guard at the door of the GPO as he had the first time I'd seen him at the door of Liberty Hall.

"Busy night, Doctor," he smiled, showing his distinct lack of teeth.

"Are you alright, Sean?"

"Fine, Sir, but I do thank you for asking."

I looked about and took in the activity. "What's Mr Clarke organizing?" I asked. "I see he's quite occupied."

"Oh, he's putting together his own fire brigade. Try to keep us from burning like those buildings out there. I'll take the guard, thank you. Never could see running into burning buildings." He paused to look outside again. "Men coming in," he called. A dozen or more men flushed through the door like quail in the light of a grass fire.

"That's everybody but the boys at the Metropole," shouted someone.

Pearse appeared by my side and started dividing the newcomers up. Some were sent to move explosives to the basement to better protect them from the shelling. Others were detailed to join a party already in the basement trying to construct a tunnel under Henry Street to the buildings on the north side of the road. At least, I thought, they are finally thinking of escape. But escape to where? We were completely surrounded. Maybe, if they could go under Henry Street then up and through the buildings along Moore Street, then out at Great Britain Street and away. Yes, it could work .... if the Army could be drawn closer to the GPO and the Volunteers came out behind them. But the badly wounded couldn't go, that was certain.

"You're right, doctor. The whole thing is foolish!"

"What? Oh, Collins."

"You're quiet transparent you know. You're thoughts I mean. We'll make a try tomorrow. Pearse and Connelly have been working on a plan for an escape from our little box, but you and I both know it's too late."

"I just hope we won't waste lives."

"So do I, Doctor. Next time we won't. Next time we'll know more and we'll fight on the move." He paused and looked around. "Yes, next time." He walked off and I thought about having a seat on my favourite mail sacks. But first, one more round through the infirmary.

Chapter 17

Friday

28 April 1916

I had again been unable to sleep, so I made continuous rounds. The men worked desperately, but the upper floors were now burning steadily. Try as they would, spots were put out only at great risk. The men exposed themselves to the intermittent fire of the snipers to slow the flames. For the moment at least, the cannon were quiet. Finally I succumbed to age and lack of sleep. Having made one last check of the ward, I barely remember laying back on my mail sacks in the darkness as men passed and smoke started to fill one's lungs from the burning street.

"Today, there will be an end to it." Holmes's voice came to me as if in a dream. I rolled over on my mail sacks and tried to find a more comfortable position.

"Come, come, Doctor. You've been sleeping for almost three hours; it's time to get up and about."

"Holmes, what the devil are you doing back?" I rubbed my eyes and sat up.

"There will be an end of things today, I think. By tomorrow at the latest. New man is in charge, General Sir John Maxwell."

"I thought he was in Egypt."

"No, he was in England and at rather loose ends, I suppose, for he's been sent here with full powers to do whatever he thinks he should."

"And what does he think?"

"Ah, well. I was able to participate in the meeting a few hours ago. Maxwell is at the Army Headquarters in Kilmainham Hospital. He's left Lowe in charge of Dublin and has approved his method - surround and reduce."

"Well, there is no change there. It's the logical course."

"Yes," agreed Holmes, pulling on his pipe. "But there are some changes. First," he tapped his pipe on his boot, "he has signed a proclamation that he will destroy any neighbourhood or area where he finds rebels. There will be no questions. Second, he has ordered a pit dug at Arbour Hill Detention Centre."

"A pit?"

"Well, a grave, if you will, large enough to hold one hundred bodies."

"What? Surely not!"

"Think not?" Holmes pulled out his tobacco pouch.

"Well, of course I believe you, but surely he does not mean to just execute people."

"Oh, of course not, they'll get a fair trial," he lighted the pipe, "then he'll shoot them. He intends to give Pearse his blood sacrifice in spades."

I sat quietly for a few moments. "Anything else?"

"Yes, no organization shall be left to exist in the open. Not the Volunteers or the ICA, not even the Hibernian Rifles or the Foresters."

"I understand that, of course. But doesn't he realize that executions will only give them martyrs?"

"Yes, that's why he intends to bury the leaders in quick lime. No bodies!"

"What can we do?"

"The same as we've done, old fellow, try to keep people alive as best we can. Neither side will listen to us openly.

"Everything is fairly well situated as far as Lowe and Maxwell are concerned. The GPO will be the big push come dawn. The rest they'll just hold in place." He continued to puff on his lighted pipe.

Struggling off my bags, I suddenly felt old. "I'm sure there'll be some tea in the other room, Liam. I need some."

"Of course, Thomas, I could do with some as well." We had just entered the makeshift kitchen when the first cannon of the morning fired and the building shook. I looked Holmes in the eye. "I'm getting my tea!" I asserted.

"As I, Doctor," grinned Holmes.

I took a china cup from one of the ladies, thanked her, and drank hastily as another round hit the upper floors.

"Come, Thomas, it's time to see if we can intervene." Putting down his cup, Holmes walked toward the Public Office while I swallowed the last of my tea and hastened to follow. Between the fall of shell, was the buzz of the machine guns like thousands of bees telling us to leave.

Connolly was on a new cot, this one with casters. Two ICA men were pushing him about as he continued to direct the construction of defences. I peeped out the windows to see all the buildings around us burning or already smouldering bulks. The streets themselves were littered with debris and devoid of human life. It was too dangerous even for the looters. One saving grace was the large amount of ammunition the soldiers were wasting on empty buildings as everything had now been abandoned except for our own position. I despaired at the scene before me. Leaving my vantage point, I went to where Holmes stood talking with Connolly, Pearse, and Plunkett. It was a surreal scene I would have expected out of some novel by Mr Wells. A man on a mattress, one on a cot, a dreamer and a spy, all arguing the fate of hundreds of people - none but the spy knowing, or should I say, admitting, the truth of the situation. It was Holmes who was speaking as I approached.

"Boss, if we don't get out now, we're goin' to get run over like Custer at the Little Bighorn."

"I appreciate your opinion, Liam, but we can hold out a while yet, and the longer, the better," replied Pearse. "The men are doing quite well."

"The men will do what you and Mr Connolly ask, Mr Pearse, which gives you a responsibility I wouldn't want." Holmes turned to Connolly, "And you, sir, the doctor here says you gotta get to a hospital or you'll be dead. Then what good will you be to your men?" We all looked, involuntarily, at his leg. "And Mr Plunkett there, he should be in the hospital too."

There was a pause before Connolly replied. "No, Liam, I know your council is well meant, but we're all right for now. I think the fires are under control for the moment and they're not in a position to rush us yet."

"But the fires are getting worse up above, sir. I've been up there."

"At least send the women out, for God's sake, man." I interposed. "We can't have them here when the end comes."

"I can see you don't know our women, Doctor. There will be hell to pay to force them to leave. They won't do it willingly." Taking a deep breath, Connolly was thoughtful for a moment. If I could get Pearse alone, I thought, we might make the evacuation happen, or even surrender.

"We're staying and that's the end of it. At least for now." Clarke had come up behind without my notice. He was a stern figure. Though slight and somewhat bookish looking, his presence was one that was felt. His quiet spoke more than a thousand books. His would be a force I knew I could not overcome, but try I would. "And the women and wounded?"

"We'll deal with that in due course."

"Sir, the King's forces are within a few hundred yards of us in all directions."

"True," replied Clarke, "and we haven't been able to tunnel under Henry Street, but for now at least, we stay here."

211

"If you don't act, the deaths of women and boys will be on your soul not the souls of the soldiers who are without!"

With that, I stormed off to the infirmary, leaving all behind save Holmes, who nodded to the group and followed. I consoled myself that I had done my best. While Holmes left for the upper floors to make another assessment, I once again made my rounds and talked to each man. Father Flanagan was also making round of each man in our little ward, hearing confessions, giving absolutions and stuffing notes from the men to their loved ones in what must have been pockets that reached to his knees. He held a constant smile. Every man got a hearty handshake, a quick prayer, and assurance that messages would be delivered. How he would be able to get out safely any more than we would I could not see. Perhaps the stovepipe hat would be his safe passage.

It was just before noon when the O'Rahilly brought our prisoners up from the cellar to feed them and then send them back below for their own protection. Among them were the men from the Bank of Ireland. One, a man named Harry Pepper, was talking to our friend, Sean Duffy, who evidently had been detailed to the guard mount. In a moment the two of them approached me as I was bandaging another volunteer with burns.

"This prisoner wants to address you, Doctor. Is that all right?"

"Surely, Sean." I looked up at him from my work. "What is it Pepper? Are you ill?"

"No, sir." He held his hat in his hand; his eyes looked down toward his boots. "It's this, Doctor. These men here have treated us right and we've always been with them in their cause." He glanced up and then back down at his boots. "It's just, well, we got caught up in the other thing, you know. We got selfish like, and we know there's going to be consequences but right now we want to help." He looked back at me with a pleading face. "All of us do, sir. We'll give our parole and take what's coming. But for now, couldn't we be let up to help?"

I scrutinized the man's face. I believed him, I didn't trust him, but I believed him.

"I'll do this, Pepper; I'll speak on your behalf. I'll recommend you be allowed to help, unarmed, in fighting the fires or working with me. I promise nothing else."

"That's fine, sir. I trust you to do your best. Me and the boys appreciate it."

"Take him back to his friends in the basement, Sean. I'll let you know what's decided."

By now the fires were growing worse. To touch the walls of the building meant burning your hands. Still, men and women went about their tasks: nursing, cooking, fighting the fire that surrounded us from four sides and above, and returning shot for shot to the snipers at the Gresham Hotel. In three wars now I had seen such bravery. How sad.

Holmes returned from above. "Hopeless, Doctor. They'll never put out the fire."

"And evacuation?"

"Connolly has agreed. The women must go. They're to gather here and be sent out under a white flag."

"Will it be honoured?"

"One can only hope."

It was Pearse who assembled the women. It was perhaps 30 girls that crowded around. MacDiarmada and Fitzgerald were with him as he addressed the assembled. He looked at them and smiled. He looked more like a kindly priest than a combat leader.

"When the history of this week is written, the highest honours will be paid you. You have taken part in the greatest armed attempt to liberate Ireland since 1798. You obeyed the order to come here. Now I ask you to obey a more difficult one."

There was a sudden chorus of "No" shouted from the assembled women. "What was all that stuff about equality?" cried a lady in the back.

Pearse had been ready for the discord. He held up his hand and looked about until quiet prevailed. In a slow, well-modulated voice, he continued. "I am not asking you, but telling you to leave. I know it's not easy and some of you might be shot. But you showed your readiness for that when you came. Now go and God be with you."

The women were not at all happy with the decision. Neither was MacDiarmada, who pulled Pearse over by me and in a whisper argued against sending the women out. But Pearse was firm.

Fitzgerald went over by the door and called for order and a white flag, which he gave to one of the girls. Fitzgerald, like the O'Rahilly, had been against the rising, but once started felt it his duty to participate. He had spent the week in charge of stores and the kitchen, and so in close contact with many of the ladies he was about to send out. His concern for them was obvious. I too, feared for those who had helped me so.

"You heard the order ladies," cried Fitzgerald sternly.

A white flag secured, it was given to the first lady in line and tentatively held out the door. The firing started to quiet and the ladies, all save three, exited into the street as the machine guns fell silent. Connolly's secretary, Winifred Carney, and two others, Grenan and O'Farrell, refused to go.

We all waited, silent, expectant, until the ladies were brought behind the British barricade. Whatever their fate, they were at least out of harm's way. The street remained silent for a few moments until a single shot from way of the Gresham renewed the onslaught of bullets.

"We've made some progress, eh, Thomas?" Holmes was now hopeful that the surrender would not be far off.

"Some," I replied, "but now they've less reason to quit."

"The women's surrender worked, why not the rest?" He seemed puzzled by my comment.

"Warfare doesn't work logically all the time old fellow.

You box. It goes against man's nature to give up in a fight. They know they're down, but they'll go on for a while yet."

"Lunch, Gentlemen." It was Fitzgerald calling. "It may be our last here so we've a fine chicken dinner."

"But it's Friday," replied a volunteer.

We walked into what had been the mess for the last week and there before us was a mountain of food, perhaps the best some had ever seen. In the centre of plenty lay platters of freshly cooked chicken. The men looked at it but no one would touch it. That is, until Father Flanagan, knowing the men needed to eat, stepped forward. While everyone watched, he retrieved a piece of the fowl and with great zest, bit down. The men started to cheer and eat a hearty meal. He had given them dispensation to eat meat by action instead of word. All the while, the shooting continued. I joined in the meal. One thing the army had taught me was to eat when the opportunity presented itself. Who knew where the next meal would come from or when? Holmes, of course, satisfied himself with another pipe instead.

"You really should eat, Liam."

"Yes, I know, but I'm satisfied with this. You however, want to ask me something."

"No, just tell you that I've need of help in the ward and our four friends of the other night have offered their assistance. I'm going to take them up on it. Objections?"

"None."

"Indeed? I thought…"

"No, Watson, I've no need to see them punished in a formal court. With Burns dead, they'll return to their old ways, perhaps, or they may use this to find their own redemption."

"But surely you've reported the whole episode to the DMP. They'll want these men."

"Why report anything? No, the right people know and the Castle does not want it known that one of their own used this whole unfortunate occurrence." Standing, Holmes started to the front of the building. "Use them as you want, old fellow."

I had to admit it all seemed the best way out, so I went in search of Pearse to whom I explained my need to use our four friends below. To this he readily agreed. With his permission I sent for Pepper and the others. Duffy brought them up for me. They were somewhat dejected looking in their stolen IV uniforms but listened attentively as I explained their situation.

"Mr Pepper has told me you all wish to make amends for your recent actions by assisting here as you can. I'm going to give you that chance. Here are your choices. Work here with me caring for the wounded or return below as a prisoner. If you choose to help, when this is over, you'll be free to go your own way as far as we're concerned. However, should you claim you want to help and then in any way try to betray us or to run off, you will be found and dealt with." I paused and looked in the eyes of each man. "Do we understand each other?"

As I looked from face to face, each man nodded.

Pepper stepped forward. "We're all with you, sir. We want to help with the good work. It's our country too."

"All right then. Ryan," I called. "take these four men if you'd be so kind and assign them duties as you need."

"Of course, Doctor. This way men. We've plenty to do. You two men go over to Captain Mahoney, you other two stay with me."

I went to find Holmes. He was on the first floor from where he could see the streets burning from the river to the Pro-Cathedral. Even the Metropole across the street was fully engulfed in flames. Men were everywhere fighting the flames. While Pearse tried to make cohesion out of chaos, he had not the force to make it work. The O'Rahilly was the one who now directed the overall attack on the flames as Clarke and MacDiarmada tried to organize the use of hoses. While the fire took control, men continued the fight at the barricaded windows to keep the British foe at bay. The fire was now in the lift shafts, spreading from basement to roof. We all knew there was no hope.

"We'll be done by nightfall, Watson. The fire hoses have burned away. There's little water pressure and the roof and the second floor are abandoned. The soldiers won't come. They only have to wait for us to come out."

"That's why I've come, Holmes. I could use some help when we get ready to evacuate. I've got about two dozen wounded. Litter cases and walking and you've been in and out of Jervis Hospital. Can you lead us through?"

"Of course, old fellow. Let's go see what we have, shall we?"

218

Together we descended to the ground floor and through the chaos of 400 men trying to battle the enemy without and the fire within. It was young Ryan who informed me that we were to get the wounded fit to move by sunset. Mr Fitzgerald had been put in charge of evacuating the wounded and was off drafting men to be litter bearers.

"This will be difficult, Thomas. It's not easy to get to Jervis through the tunnel, but we'll make do," declared Holmes. Spying our former prisoners, he left me to supervise them in constructing litters suitable for our coming journey. Ryan, Mahoney, and I revisited each wounded man, doing what we could to ready them. So the rest of the afternoon proceeded as each floor was abandoned and the few rooms left to us crowded with men.

It was half seven when the O'Rahilly brought our prisoners up from the basement. Lieutenant Chalmers was the senior man among them. He was addressed by the O'Rahilly as they stood near the door to Henry Street.

"It's up to you now, Lieutenant. You and your men can stay with us while we remain or you can take this white flag and leave now. The choice is yours. You and your men are safe from us in either case." The O'Rahilly was a sight to see. His hair was scorched and his eyebrows burned away from fighting fire. As he talked he had men moving the explosives from the basement to a small concrete room near the ward. And while confusion reigned, Father O'Flanagan was checking on the wounded as if he were strolling about his parish yard. What a strange scene.

"We're out," said Chalmers. Taking the hand of each man, the O'Rahilly wished them luck and the Lieutenant led out, white flag held high. In a moment, they were gone down Henry Street then up Moore Lane toward their own barricades. Later I would learn that the Lieutenant had been wounded and one man killed, shot down by their own men.

I went to the O'Rahilly. "What now, Sir? What is the plan?"

"We try to go north, through the barricade on Moore Street. There's a factory on Great Britain Street which will do well for us. Then we'll try to link up with Ned Daly at the Four Courts. At least, that's the plan."

"But the wounded?"

"I believe MacDiarmada has told young Ryan to get them ready. You can take them to Jervis as best you can." He looked out toward the Henry Street door. "Connolly and Plunkett will be coming with us."

"But that's madness. Connolly has to get to hospital. Besides, the two of them will only hamper the escape of the rest."

The O'Rahilly shook his head. "We've little enough chance of getting out. Besides, the men love Connolly. He's better off with us. Don't worry, Doctor. It'll all be fine." And so saying he walked toward the door. I returned to our little ward where Mahoney and Ryan had things well in hand.

Here we had a short conference. It was decided that the

three of us would go with the wounded and would return if possible. Father O'Flanagan was coming too but the three women would go with the main body: Carney, Grenan and O'Farrell, would go with the main body in their attempt to escape. There was no dissuading them.

Holmes and our four friends were busy making litters from anything handy - blankets, thin mattresses, whatever was at hand - while all around us fire and debris fell from above. And still the artillery threw cannon shot into the upper floors, each shot drowning us with burning timber. Under Fitzgerald's guidance, we organized our evacuation, most badly injured first behind Holmes, who knew the route, then the less severely injured. Ryan, Mahoney, and I would spread ourselves out to deal with emergencies.

"All right," said Fitzgerald, "we move as soon as the O'Rahilly takes out the advance party. Are we ready?"

"Yes," was all I could think to say. Holmes, Fitzgerald, and I went to Henry Street door. The O'Rahilly was to take about 30 men with him. He was rising from his knees in front of Father Flanagan when I saw him. He had received absolution. He bid the good father farewell and took out his Peter the Painter. Looking about at those who were praying for him, he shouted, "Cheerio," but Pearse stopped him. Not a word passed between the two men as they shook hands. The O'Rahilly now stepped back, looking at his 30 men. "Now!" he yelled and they flooded out the door behind him.

"Time to go Doctor." It was Fitzgerald calling. Holmes was already through the back wall of the GPO and men were passing litters through one at a time. Passing behind one of the litters, I entered through a hole of broken brick to the house beyond. A hand reached out to pull me through and another grabbed my elbow. I looked up into the smiling face of Cacy. "Here you go, Doctor. On to the far wall and keep your head down under the window as you go past." He reached for the litter behind me. I crossed two small rooms and found myself at the next tunnel. Here I stopped to help Pepper manhandle two litters through. I had almost gotten use to the smoke-filled buildings, but now the extra exertions made my lungs burn. I went on behind the last of the litters as Pepper continued to help the walking wounded. We passed across some type of shop up a stairway and out onto a roof. There we bent low for Moore Street was straight north of where we gathered. Above us was a ladder to a door leading into the Coliseum Variety Theatre. The litter cases were in agony as they were tied to their litters and handed up and in through the door. I scrambled up the ladder. As each man arrived, Ryan, Mahoney or I checked for re-opened wounds. It had taken almost a half-hour to move half a block and the fire was following us.

Here Fitzgerald decided to rest for a bit. We had no sooner laid the men on the carpet when a runner arrived asking for Captain Mahoney. Connolly's protective cage, over his leg, had been damaged. Could he come back and fix it? Mahoney didn't hesitate but went straight away. He was back in what seemed like moments.

It was Holmes who suggested a Red Cross flag be flown from the pole on the roof but to do so arms must be taken out.

Fitzgerald insisted that the rules of war would be followed. "We need to dump our arms back at the GPO," he insisted. "Let's pile them here and two of us can take them out."

There were not more than a dozen weapons. It was with great reluctance I added my pocket pistol to the pile. That action made me involuntarily pat my vest for my letter. When I looked up, I could see Holmes smiling at me.

"Doctor Ryan." Jim Ryan was tapping me on the shoulder. "I'm going back to look after Mr Connolly. They may have real need of help when they fight through. You and the Captain have no need of me now."

I was about to volunteer to go along. "Well, I think that I...." Holmes was looking sternly at me and shaking his head ever so slightly.

"Yes, Doctor?" Ryan was appraising me quizzically.

"Oh, I was just going to say, if we don't meet again, be sure to finish medical school. You'll make a fine surgeon." I reached out my hand, the two of us shook, and he was gone out the door.

Holmes approached as I stared at the empty doorway.

"I'll have need of you, Watson. All we can do now is save what lives we can. And that will be in the offices of our friends in the khaki uniforms."

"I understand, Holmes, but I don't like letting that boy go off like that. I want him alive, not martyred."

"Yes, I know."

Cacy had approached and grabbed Holmes by the elbow. "There's no putting up a flag, Liam. It's suicide to try and get on the roof."

"Well, don't worry 'bout it. We can use it when we go out to the hospital."

"Liam, Cacy, come here." Fitzgerald was standing with Father O'Flanagan by the weapons pile.

"Yes, sir."

"Father and I are going to take these weapons back to the GPO. We'll be back in a few moments. Maybe there's someone still to take them."

"But sir, I can…" started Cacy.

"No, I want you two to find a way out of here. That fire will be here shortly and we'll need to get these men out. I'm relying on you."

He bent over to pick up the stacked rifles. Slinging them over his shoulder, Father Flanagan doing the same, the two of them made an awkward retreat through the door and down the ladder. Cacy and Holmes left to find an exit that would not lead to further destruction and I went back to the wounded.

I was convinced that all would recover if given prompt attention save one who worried me. He was a slight lad who had been unconscious for the better part of the afternoon.

Fitzgerald and the priest were back quickly. The tunnels were now a conduit for the fire, and as fires do, this one was creating its own wind to force the flames toward us.

Holmes, of course, had been through the building now numerous times and knew well where the only unlocked door was. But he played the game and allowed Cacy to "discover" the only door without a padlock. Later, he would tell me there was actually a window, hidden by draperies, which he had used before. The unlocked door, which opened into a passageway, led to a locked gate that opened on to Princes Street.

There was now a scramble to find a tool to open the gate. A pickaxe was procured from where the tunnellers had worked and Cacy made haste with his trophy to open the gate.

We had now been at rest for nearly an hour. Fitzgerald insisted we must press on to the hospital. The men picked up their fellows on their make-shift stretchers with the greatest care. We started down the stairs to street level and out the unlocked door to a narrow passage. One man carried our make shift Red Cross flag in front with Father Flanagan at his side. We all followed to the edge of the passage. Here we hesitated. Prince's Street ended to the west at the wall of Arnott's Drapery Store. To the east, it opened to Sackville Street but faced the burning Imperial Hotel. So here,, though the fires lighted the sky like an artificial sun, we were able to cross with relative immunity. It was only the occasional stray bullet or shrapnel that came our way.

We crossed Princes Street and entered an alleyway partially blocked by a burning barricade of what appeared to be rolls of newspaper. We passed the wounded in their blankets over the flames and continued down a narrowing passage to Middle Abbey Street. From here we peered around the sides of the buildings. To the east a barricade of our own was in flames blocking the way to Sackville Street. To our west were Jervis Hospital and a British barricade of sandbags manned with soldiers and machine guns. And from windows all about us volunteers were trading shots with the British forces. It seemed that only the fires consuming the buildings on both sides of the street would move them.

Fitzgerald knew all too well the danger of our situation.

"All right then, hold that flag out high soldier. Listen men, we're going out and right to Jervis. Move slowly, no running, no sudden moves. We've got to make them understand that this is a mercy mission." He looked about at the faces around him. This was our most dangerous moment yet. Both sides needed to cease firing; our only hope was respect for our little flag. In a moment we would be easy prey. I sucked in my breath involuntarily and gazed at the Red Cross, so plain, in the light of the fires.

The call from Fitzgerald brought me out of my thoughts.

"Out then, boys."

We started out of the narrow passage at what seemed a snail's pace and turned right toward the hospital. Everything in me screamed "run for cover." I looked to Holmes, who was across from me helping to carry one of the stretcher victims. He merely smiled back. Somehow, that made me feel better. It was then as I staggered into the street that was lighted like noon that the firing died away. I had a sense there was a thousand angels holding their breath as we slowly passed down the pavement toward Liffey Street. Beyond stood the British sandbags. We moved without a word. The sudden silence of the guns gave an eerie feeling. One could now both feel the heat and hear flames crackle as the fire was consuming the city. We continued forward, the only sound the shuffling of feet as we picked our way through the rubble of a week of devastation.

I now wondered what had happened to the rest of the men. Were they already in the mountains? Fighting their way through to the west and south to the Four Courts? Or dead in the streets?

"Halt where you are!"

It was a shout from behind the barricade. We could see a row of rifles and a Lewis gun with nervous soldiers peering at us over the sights of their weapons. A captain and a major were off to the right in deep conversation. While they talked, they kept looking at us. They were surely wondering if this was some sort of trick. The captain sent a runner off somewhere while they conversed. It seemed forever but was probably about five minutes before the captain finally called to us.

"Man with the flag. You and the other come forward and be recognized."

Father Flanagan now had the flag and was about to start forward when Captain Mahoney's hand restrained him. "I'll go with you, Father. Maybe they'll take my word for things."

"Thank you, Captain. I surely hope they'll take the word of a man of God and one of the King."

The two started forward, but were stopped a good dozen paces short of the barricade by a command to halt.

"Holmes," I hissed, "we might…"

"No, Watson. It would just confuse the situation. Later, once we're in the hospital."

I thought that our identifying ourselves might be a boon to our situation, but as usual, Holmes was correct. I could hear a discussion between the captain and Father Flanagan and Captain Mahoney. I could not make out what they were saying from where I stood, but it was plain that the officer wasn't sure whether to believe our two representatives. The captain sent off another runner and a moment later two young men in civilian clothing appeared. The two were quite animated and pointing at Father Flanagan. Their heads bobbed up and down. The captain also nodded. With a wave from Mahoney, we picked up our burdens and moved slowly toward the side entrance to Jervis. Nuns, nurses, and medical staff poured out to help us carry the wounded inside.

"Mr Altamont," came the booming voice of the Major at the barricade, "this way for you. I remember you, sir. Spied at the Castle did you? Well, never mind, we'll take care of that."

I was near panic. If Holmes were taken this way he might be tortured or worse. I started to step toward the barricade, but Holmes laid his hand on my sleeve. "Easy old fellow, I'll be fine," said Holmes, and winked at me though he had a scowl on his face. "How do you think I've gotten back and forth," he whispered.

"Don't worry, Doctor. I'll be fine," he shouted and waved back as two soldiers grabbed him and pulled him across the sandbag wall.

I turned back to the wounded as we entered the hospital. Mahoney was still with us. He and I explained each case to the medical staff. The hospital was filled with patients - civilians, military and Volunteers. Many of the supposed civilians I knew to be Volunteers whom I had treated during the week and we had smuggled through to Jervis.

I had been there not more than 30 minutes when a soldier came into the triage room asking that I and Captain Mahoney report to the Major at the barricade. We left Father Flanagan with the wounded. I knew that Holmes was safe and I still carried my safe conduct papers, yet still I worried. That is, until I saw Holmes and the Major taking tea in a room just off the foyer of the hospital.

"Come in, Doctor, Captain. Tea?"

"Yes," I sighed as I sank into a chair. I looked at the clock on the far wall, just a bit after eleven. The end of the fifth day of the rebellion and I was still in one piece.

"Understand it was a tough go out there, Doctor."

"Yes, quite, Major. Though I suspect you haven't had a good time of it."

The Major gave a crooked smile. "No, very bad show down the road toward Kingstown. They bloodied our noses fairly badly. We've over two hundred dead and wounded. I'm told up north of town there's been a bit of a brawl too." (Later I found out he was talking about Mount St. Bridge and Ashbourne.) "But all's in hand now."

Mahoney was staring at me.

"You mean, all the time…"

"Yes, Captain," replied Holmes. "We've been working for one reason, to save lives."

"You, too?" He was incredulous, "and you sound British, not American."

"I had always found that good theatrical training is a distinct benefit in my line of work. And the Lieutenant Colonel here has been of immeasurable help, not only here, but throughout my career. Let me introduce myself. My name is Sherlock Holmes and this is my good friend, Dr John Watson of the RAMC." Holmes bowed with all the drama of an actor taking a curtain call. It was the kind of theatrics I needed. The tension was broken and I laughed until tears came to my eyes. I'm afraid my two fellow officers thought me on the edge of a nervous breakdown.

"I've heard of you, Mr Holmes. The Colonel here has written stories about you, hasn't he?"

"Ah, time has passed, Watson. I'm afraid you're not as well-known as you once were."

"That's all right. Doyle still sends me royalties enough," I quipped. We were all quiet for a moment and I sipped the tea. "What of the stretcher party?" I asked. "What becomes of them?"

"Gaol in the morning. We'll hold them here until light."

"And the women who came out?"

"Were they part of the game?"

"I don't think so," I lied, "pressed into service."

"Well, we'll see."

"And Father O'Flanagan?"

"Ah, well, unless he actively fought, we dare not hold a priest. We'd surely have a rising over that. No, he'll be sent on his way."

"Good." I looked to Holmes. "I'm afraid I'm suddenly a tired old fellow. Can we find a place to sleep?"

"Already arranged, Watson, but we've more to do before we sleep, old friend. We're off to see General Maxwell. Unless, of course, you'd rather not. I can go alone."

"No, Holmes. In for a penny, in for a pound."

"Yes," replied the Major, "I've a motor outside, the driver will take you to the Royal Military Hospital. I believe that's where the General is at the moment. General Lowe is to meet with him tonight. You may leave any time you wish."

Chapter 18

Saturday

29 APRIL 1916

We followed a fairly straight route to the Hospital, down Parkgate, past Kingsbridge Station, and quickly over to Army Headquarters. An occasional shot was heard in the distance, but mainly my impression was of the glow from the fire. Holmes and I sat in the town car as the driver moved swiftly down the streets.

"Holmes, what about Martha? Has she been all right? Do you know?"

"Yes, she's been in England since Monday night. I instructed her to go to Kingstown and take the ferry as soon as I sent word it had started."

"Well, thank heaven for that. You do think of everything, Holmes."

"No, old fellow, if I had thought of everything, none of this would have happened."

"Holmes, you did all you could. When the world has gone mad, one man cannot set it right."

"Thank you, Watson, but had I been able to truly get within the inner circle, things might have been different."

"If you'd been in the inner circle, the rebels might have won. Then where would we be?"

Holmes laughed for the first time in days.

The yard of the hospital was filled with soldiers. We drew up to the front door. With sidelong looks from those around and the sentries at the front, we were escorted through the halls and into a large conference room. Here we found a half-dozen staff officers.

On the table before them was a map of the city and in it were pins of various colours. The arrangement of the map was almost identical to that which the rebels had used a week before. Interesting, I thought, how all armies worked so alike. The wall clock was striking one as Maxwell looked up from his study of the maps in front of him.

"Ah, you must be the spies I've been told to expect. Well, what have you?"

Holmes bristled instantly. I could see the change in him as he stood straighter and his eyes pierced at the general. Maxwell was not an easy man to deal with and he obviously did not relish his position. He had a hard reputation in Egypt as to his dealings with the natives, and I instantly saw that his attitude toward the Irish would be no different.

Lowe, who I much more respect to this day, stepped up.

"General, let me introduce Mr Sherlock Holmes, the consulting detective. He has spent almost two years in working within the Shinners organization for us. You might remember the Von Bork Affair? It was Mr Holmes who solved that situation for us. And this is Lieutenant Colonel John Watson of the RAMC. He was recently brought in to assist Mr Holmes."

At the mention of Von Bork and then being told I was an Army man, Maxwell seemed to relax a bit. Like most military men, he took a dim view of civilians and spies were to be loathed. But, Holmes was proven and I was one of his own so he would listen to what Holmes had to say.

Holmes gave a quick overview of the week. He told them of his estimate of the strength of the men who had abandoned the GPO, of their northerly course, and their intent to double around to the Four Courts.

"Connolly is a litter case you say? Well, they're cornered in some buildings not two blocks from the GPO from what we can tell. They certainly haven't broken through our lines." Maxwell walked back to the table and once again inspected the map.

"I see no reason to rush in, Lowe. Your strategy seems to have done well so far. No waste of men or equipment. We'll make the beggars come to us. With the countryside generally quiet, we can continue to concentrate."

"Dr Watson, what's the prognosis on Connolly?"

"He'll need a hospital or he'll be dead in a few days. That's as plain as I can say it."

"He'll be dead in a few days anyway. And their will to fight, Mr Holmes?"

"Connolly and Clarke would just as soon fight to the death, which they might do if left to themselves. But they've made Pearse the Commander and he'll surrender so that you can

234

kill him. Martyrdom appeals to him."

"We'll have no martyrs, but there will be payment for this. When I'm through, no one will think of doing it again for a hundred years."

I was amazed at the contradictions in his statement that he himself seemed to be unaware of. The man had no concept of where his thinking would take a country that had re-awakened to its identity.

"Come, Watson. It's time for us to exit the stage. This play for us is done." My friend looked tired but his eyes told me that he had something in mind.

Lowe came over and shook our hands. "Your information has been a great help, Mr Holmes, and saved many lives."

"I'm afraid it has not saved this island for the Union, sir, and I regret that. I will be returning to London tomorrow. Dr Watson, I believe, will want to return to his other duties in Kent."

"Holmes, I feel as though I should stay a few days yet. They'll have need of extra hands at the Castle Hospital for a while."

"Of course, Watson. Goodbye General." He turned and we left without a word from Maxwell.

Our driver was still waiting outside. He had been instructed to take us to Ross's Hotel just next to the Royal Barracks where rooms were available to us.

We rode the short distance in silence. I thanked the young private, who drove us and entered the hotel to find that my whole kit, which I had left in London, was waiting for me.

"Yes," replied the desk clerk to my question. "It arrived about a week ago with a note that you would be calling for it, sir. The note was from Mr Mycroft Holmes. It was odd though."

"Odd? How so?"

"Well, sir, the note had the annotation that you would call this morning before five a.m. for your bags. Nothing comes into Kingsbridge Station that time of morning." The clock behind the desk said 4:30.

"Holmes, how could he know?"

"I don't know, Watson. Truly I don't."

As we walked to the stairs to go up to our rooms I could still hear firing from a short distance as it echoed between the buildings; light shown through the windows as the fire still raged.

"It's about over, Holmes."

"Yes, Watson, all but the killing."

"Maxwell will think better of it. You'll see Holmes."

"No, Watson, he won't. He'll have his pound of flesh and give Ireland away." He stopped on the stairs and took my hand. "Thank you, old friend, for helping me to try. I'll be gone in the morning when you get up. I need to see Mycroft. If anyone can influence what is to come, it is he."

236

"I won't tarry long here, Holmes. I don't think I can stand much of this."

"Good old Watson!"

He entered his room and shut the door. I entered mine and lay my head down just as the first rays of sun were over the horizon. I thought I would be unable to sleep but as soon as my head was on the pillow, I must have been dead away.

A hard pounding at my door awoke me. I had only been asleep two hours by my watch. "Coming, coming, who is it?" I opened the door. "Holmes, I thought you were leaving?"

"Yes, but I want a crack at Nathan and Birrell first. I understand they're at the Castle. Perhaps they can influence Maxwell. I doubt it but I must try. Well, come on, man. Get dressed."

I hurried a shave in cold water and donned my uniform. By just after eight o'clock we were entering the castle yard. There I was relieved to find Constable Flood. He looked much the worse for wear, but smiled as we entered.

"Joined up, have you, Doctor? Didn't recognize you for a moment, Liam, good to see you."

Flood leaned toward me and, in a conspiratorial tone, allowed as how Liam had been going in and out all week at odd times. I grinned and Flood winked back.

We made our way through a large encampment of soldiers in the courtyard, through the foyer, down the hall and into Room 6. Here sat a solitary soldier of the signal corps. He leaped up from his chair, dropping a book as we entered.

"Morning, sir. Mr Altamont. Who do you need to see, sir?" Holmes instructed him as to our need to see Birrell and Nathan. The young man departed.

I looked at the title on the book. "*A Tourist Guide to Ireland.*" I noted. "At least the young man wants to see something of the countryside."

"Let's hope he doesn't have to do it with a rifle, Watson."

When the two men who had run Irish Affairs for so long entered Room 6, I was shocked. Rarely had I seen such an utter change in men. The two had the look of men under the gallows, which, I suppose, in a way they were. They were haggard and drawn. Nathan especially had the hollow eyes of one who has sat in the trench during long hours of shelling. They knew that their careers had gone up in flames with the city, a city that they truly loved but could not protect. They now realized they had been doomed from the time that the Ulster Volunteers had formed, the officers of the Curragh had mutinied, and the government in England had failed to act. They are where the Fates have dictated. The three hags must have laughed at their work.

"You bring what word, Mr Holmes," asked Nathan.

"We all know, sir, that this rebellion is all but over. What I have to ask is about your status and that of Mr Birrell. Do either of you have any influence with Maxwell?"

"Ah, as to that Mr Holmes," Birrell sat heavily behind the table, "I'm sure you know the answer to your own question. We have neither control nor influence over the man." He looked up at Nathan, and then continued. "He thinks us fools of the worst order. If it were up to him, we too would be tried and executed. He's no use for civil authority. He is in charge, and, unless replaced, will not even listen to the Prime Minister. No," he lowered his head and looked at his hands. "No, Matthew and I will be sacrificed on the altar of government and sent away with all the blame, whether it is ours or not. Whatever your idea Mr Holmes, we cannot help you."

"Fair enough, sir. I appreciate your candour. I'll leave on the mail boat and hope to be in London tonight. Watson, you won't come with me?"

"No, Holmes. I'm off to the ward to see what's to be done."

Holmes thanked the two men and we left them, silent and morose, in the quiet of the room.

I said goodbye to Holmes at the foyer and we parted company. He was off to Kingstown and I to the hospital ward. It was barely half ten in the morning.

The wards were filled, not only with our patients from the Great War, but also patients from our little one. The entire Castle, with its few hundred soldiers and patients had been on short rations. Only now was food starting to come through. Medical supplies I found rich in abundance, compared to my work of the last week. I was heartily welcomed back by the staff that was curious about both my absence and my new status. To their enquiries I merely replied that I had been on a special assignment for a short time as I would need to return to Kent and my usual work.

It was at rounds in the early afternoon that word spread like wildfire. The Rebels were surrendering! Cheers resounded through the Castle, but now, I thought, we must deal with the aftermath. Some of that aftermath was not long in coming. About mid-afternoon I was drinking tea and looking out the window toward the courtyard. There was quite a commotion at the gate. Seven of Connolly's men had carried him to the Castle and asked that he be put in the hospital. I rushed, unthinking, to the gate. Connolly was the first to recognize me as I bent down to check his leg.

"Ah, Doctor, you seem to have changed sides."

"No, sir, I've always been on the side of reason." I stared into his eyes.

"Well said."

"The leg?"

"Not so bad as it could be."

"We'll get it properly treated now. You'll be all right." I wasn't at all sure of that myself and I could tell he didn't believe me anyway.

"Bloody Hell! It's Doctor Ryan!" The outburst came from Sean Duffy who stood half at attention by Connolly. He had helped to carry him in.

I stood up. "Hello, Duffy. It's actually Dr Watson."

"And I thought…"

"I'm glad you're all right Duffy. I was worried about you."

"Not likely!"

"Believe it or not, my friend, I was."

"I think," said Connolly, "it would be best if you did not attend to me Doctor. I'm sure there are others here who can help."

"I understand, sir." I stiffened a bit. "You're probably right. Good luck, sir, and may I shake the hand of a brave man?"

He hesitated a moment then lifted his hand. Without a word, we shook and I left. Connolly was taken to the old Royal Suite away from the hospital wards. I was never to see him again.

By late afternoon word had filtered down; Pearse was a prisoner at Arbour Hill and he and Connolly had both signed a surrender. Daly and the men at the Four Courts had marched in and the girl Elizabeth O'Farrell was being used to carry the surrender message to the other garrisons.

The night grew strangely silent. It was queer not to hear the guns that had fired all week. Lowe's forces had been told to stand fast, so now there came only the rare sound of a single sniper. I chose to spend the night at the Castle, immersed in treating the wounded. Somehow, there was relief in that work. I did not want to think of the men who I felt I had abandoned.

241

When I finally lay down on a cot, I could not sleep. I knew there were men out there who didn't even know that their leaders had surrendered. What would happen in the morning?

Chapter 19

30 April 1916

Sunday

By dawn, which was about a quarter to five, the entire Castle was swarming with messengers coming and going. I was sent for and asked to see Major Price over in Room 6.

"Ah, Doctor, thanks for coming. We have need of you. Could you come with me to the Rotunda Hospital? We are identifying the leaders among those that have surrendered. Since you were on the inside, your assistance would be greatly appreciated."

A chill went down me as Price made what should have been a simple request.

"No, Major, I don't believe I can be of any assistance to you. I'm sure your G-men are more than capable of identifying the leaders."

Price appraised me rather quizzically for a moment, then shrugged. "All right, Doctor. But, speaking of G-men, do you know where Sergeant Burns is? We've looked for him for days. I thought he might have made contact with you or Mr Holmes."

"I have no idea where he might be now." I was truthful about that. "I can honestly say, the last time I saw him he was fine. But that was the first day of the rebellion. I haven't seen him since."

Price stared at me. As our eyes locked I could tell he thought I was either lying or at least not telling all that I knew.

"Right, then. Thank you, Doctor. Do you know if Mr Holmes will be returning?"

"I'm afraid I don't know that either," I smiled.

"Well, no matter. We've plenty to do for the moment."

With that I went back to the wards.

All day word of more surrenders came in. Miss O'Farrell was sent into the most dangerous areas, sometimes alone, sometimes with the help of one of the priests.

It was two in the afternoon when I saw the Countess for the first time in a week. She and Mallin had marched the Citizen's Army men who had fought at St. Stephen's Green and the College of Surgeons to the Castle in surrender. Even in defeat, she held herself like a queen, unbowed and unbroken. I never got the opportunity to talk to her, for no sooner had they arrived than she and Mallin were put in a lorry and taken to Kilmainham Gaol. The men were marched off toward Richmond Barracks.

By evening, it was over. All the outlying units had surrendered. Men were already being loaded into cattle boats to be taken to England or Wales and prison. The leaders had been separated out and were spread among the local gaols. I stayed in the wards and did the only thing I knew to do.

Late in the evening I walked to O'Connell Bridge and north, across the Liffey. The fire brigade was once more out and doing what they could. The streets were filled with curious onlookers. It had almost the feel of a macabre carnival. People were picking through the ashes either for souvenirs or anything of value. Soldiers were everywhere but interfered little with the crowd and once more the DMP were on the streets. The second city of the empire was a smouldering ruin.

I walked on to the GPO. After fire, artillery and a week of fighting, there she stood above the pediment, Hibernia with her spear and harp. To her left and right were Fidelity and Mercury. The three still stood guard. I could not help but feel that this was a sign. Ireland still stood, faithful to her cause, proclaiming it to the world. I shook myself. I was becoming morose. Afghanistan, South Africa, Ireland; I was suddenly very tired of the fighting.

I walked back along Middle Abbey Street and West past Jervis Hospital - past the barricade that had stopped us just the day before - still manned but now allowing anyone to pass. I walked past the back of the Four Courts and the Royal Barracks and turned into Ross's. Stopping only for my key I went straight to my room. There were plenty of other doctors in Dublin. Tomorrow I would go to London and then on to Kent. I must see what Holmes had been able to accomplish. Yes, I thought, tomorrow I go home.

Chapter 20

1 May – 13 May 1916

I was delayed one day from my intended departure. I've no doubt it was intentional. Price was still trying to find Burns and he believed I knew something about the disappearance. Burn's body was identified on the first of May by fellow G-men. He'd had no identification on him when he went to raid the bank, so his body was placed with other dead Shinners to be looked at later. His death was put down as an accident of war.

It was now the second of May and I was determined to leave.

I took the mid-day ferry from Kingstown. I had nothing but the uniform I wore, my few things in a Gladstone and my medical bag.

I had made it a point to make a last round at the Castle and to say good-bye to Flood. It's interesting that it is always the common man who most fascinates me. He was a good man and I wished him well. I had no desire to see Maxwell, Lowe, Price, or any of the key players in our theatre of the absurd. Nathan saw me leaving. When I told him I was off to London, he wished me well. I did the same to him. For a moment I thought the man mad as he grinned and started to laugh.

"Ah, Doctor. We'll be joining you soon. Birrell and I will have to resign and I suspect Wimbourne will also be made to go. Though, in fairness, he was more right than I, but when it's a question of the government standing, they'll need to make a clean sweep of it all. Best of luck to you, Doctor. I've got to get with the arrest list."

"Arrest list?"

"Well, we can't let men like MacNeill get away."

"But he didn't fight. He tried to stop the uprising."

"No matter, he was involved and that's all that will count. We've got a few hundred around the country to get. I'm afraid we may have more fighting yet."

"What will happen to Pearse and the others?"

"Now, Doctor, you know the answer to that."

"He never even fired a pistol!"

"Those who led are the most guilty." He looked down at his boots. "Or maybe it's those who failed to lead." He seemed to drift off in thought for a moment. "Well, anyway, good luck to you Doctor." He offered his hand and we shook and parted. I felt more regret over Nathan than any of the others.

By nightfall I was in London and fortunate enough to find a hotel room. Though it was late, I planned on making a visit to the Diogenes Club to find Mycroft and perhaps Sherlock. I had much I wanted to talk about with them. I found the two brothers in Mycroft's makeshift war room. Both had obviously used the room to its named purpose. The antagonism was palpable.

The Strangers Room was a bee hive of activity. Men

were moving pins on maps of France and Turkey; telegraphers were busy sending messages; the teletype rattled. Nowhere was there a map or sign of Ireland.

It was Sherlock who saw me first and waved a hand to Mycroft's closet. Taking his brother by the arm, he moved him inside.

"Close the door, will you, Watson? Thank you."

"Ah, Doctor, I thought you'd stay a few days," remarked Mycroft, placing himself in the chair behind the desk.

"I doubt that," I replied. "You knew I had no stomach for what's coming." Sherlock smirked as Mycroft looked up through his bushy eyebrows. "No, Doctor, you're right. I didn't think you'd stay."

"Has it started?"

"By dawn, the first will be done."

"Who?"

"Pearse, Clarke, and MacDonagh."

"And there will be more?"

"Oh, undoubtedly Doctor. This needs to be ended for the duration of the war in Europe at the least. We can't be distracted by wars inside our own borders. I should think a half-dozen or so will do."

"Holmes," I turned to Sherlock, "Is there nothing we can do?"

"I'm afraid the blood lust is up in England, Watson, at

least among the politicians. They won't listen to me or Mycroft."

"But surely, Mycroft, you see what the result will be? More martyrs, more songs, more stories. Spank them yes, and then send them home like little boys. People will laugh at them. If you kill even a half dozen you'll make them heroes."

"Doctor, just because they ask my advice doesn't mean that they'll take it. The great politicians are looking a little foolish to the world right now. They want to regain control with an iron fist and let the world know they are not to be trifled with."

"Surely they know that this will cause problems with the United States."

"True, but not with the companies selling munitions and war goods. There is too much money to be made to let a little trifle in Ireland upset sales. We may be unpopular with the common man, but the common man doesn't sell artillery shells."

I sat in the chair by the right of the desk. There was an intense sadness in my soul.

"What of Casement?" I asked.

"He will be hanged, surely. Your friend, Doyle, is trying to help him. Evidently they are great friends but the Crown Prosecutor won't let Sir Roger live. There are things about the man neither you nor Doyle know. Casement will be destroyed."

I looked beseechingly to Holmes. "Sherlock?"

"Watson, I've been to the Prime Minister himself. I fear it's time two old men went home."

Denouement

I read of the first executions the next morning as I was boarding the train for Kent. The newsboys were hawking the headlines as Holmes and I walked toward the platform.

"You should come stay with me for a few days, Watson. Martha would like to see you, now that we're out of character."

"Thank you, Holmes, I'd like to take you up on that in a month or two. Right now, I think it's best to get back to my patients. The work will do me good."

"Yes, I think it will, Watson."

We walked on to where my train waited.

"We stopped a bank robbery and we kept innocent men from being blamed for it. We made the best effort we could to stop unnecessary bloodshed. You saved the lives of wounded men." Holmes shrugged and put his hand on my shoulder. "We did what we could Watson. But both sides were against us."

"Perhaps after the war is over, some solution can be found."

"Good old Watson."

"I'm not giving up on it, Holmes."

"Nor will I."

We shook hands. Without another word I boarded the first class carriage.

I watched from the window of the train as it pulled out of the station. Holmes had already turned and was walking away. I meant to keep my promise and see him again.

By the twelfth of May, Maxwell had finished his executions. In all, with Casement, sixteen would be shot or hanged. Ireland had its new martyrs, England would have more wars, and Holmes and I would be called for again.

Also from Kieran McMullen

"Exciting, and full of authentic military detail"

Sherlock Holmes Society of London

Also from MX Publishing

Close To Holmes

A Look at the Connections Between Historical London, Sherlock Holmes and Sir Arthur Conan Doyle.

Eliminate The Impossible

An Examination of the World of Sherlock Holmes on Page and Screen.

The Norwood Author

Arthur Conan Doyle and the Norwood Years (1891 - 1894) – Winner of the 2011 Howlett Literary Award (Sherlock Holmes book of the year)

www.mxpublishing.com

Also From MX Publishing

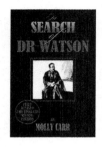

In Search of Dr Watson

Wonderful biography of
Dr. Watson from expert Molly
Carr – 2nd edition fully updated.

Arthur Conan Doyle, Sherlock
Holmes and Devon

A Complete Tour Guide and
Companion.

The Lost Stories of Sherlock Holmes

Eight more stories from the pen of John
H Watson – compiled by Tony
Reynolds.

www.mxpublishing.com

Also From MX Publishing

Watsons Afghan Adventure

Fascinating biography of Watson's
time in Afghanistan from US Army
veteran Kieran McMullen.

Shadowfall

Sherlock Holmes, ancient relics and
demons and mystic characters. A
supernatural Holmes pastiche.

Official Papers of The Hound of
The Baskervilles

Very unusual collection of the
original police papers from The
Hound case.

www.mxpublishing.com

Also From MX Publishing

The Sign of Fear

The first adventure of the 'female Sherlock Holmes'. A delightful fun adventure with your favourite supporting Holmes characters.

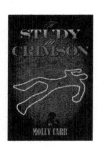

A Study in Crimson

The second adventure of the 'female Sherlock Holmes' with a host of sub-plots and new characters joining Watson and Fanshaw

The Chronology of Arthur Conan Doyle

The definitive chronology used by historians and libraries worldwide.

www.mxpublishing.com

Also From MX Publishing

Aside Arthur Conan Doyle

A collection of twenty stories from ACD's close friend Bertram Fletcher Robinson.

Bertram Fletcher Robinson

The comprehensive biography of the assistant plot producer of The Hound of The Baskervilles

Wheels of Anarchy

Reprint and introduction to Max Pemberton's thriller from 100 years ago. One of the first spy thrillers of its kind.

www.mxpublishing.com

Also From MX Publishing

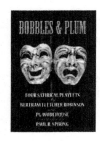

Bobbles and Plum

Four playlets from PG Wodehouse 'lost' for over 100 years – found and reprinted with an excellent commentary

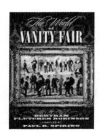

The World of Vanity Fair

A specialist full-colour reproduction of key articles from Bertram Fletcher Robinson containing of colour caricatures from the early 1900s.

Tras Las He huellas de Arthur Conan Doyle (in Spanish)

Un viaje ilustrado por Devon.

www.mxpublishing.com

Also From MX Publishing

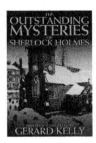

The Outstanding Mysteries of
Sherlock Holmes

With thirteen Homes stories and
illustrations Kelly re-creates the
gas-lit, fog-enshrouded world of
Victorian London

Rendezvous at The Populaire

Sherlock Holmes has retired,
injured from an encounter with
Moriarty. He's tempted out of
retirement for an epic battle with
the Phantom of the opera.

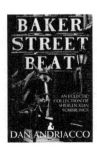

Baker Street Beat

An eclectic collection of articles,
essays, radio plays and 'general
scribblings' about Sherlock Holmes
from Dr.Dan Andriacco.

www.mxpublishing.com

Also From MX Publishing

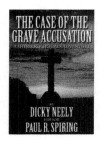

The Case of The Grave Accusation

The creator of Sherlock Holmes has been accused of murder. Only Holmes and Watson can stop the destruction of the Holmes legacy.

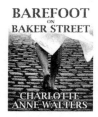

Barefoot on Baker Street

Epic novel of the life of a Victorian workhouse orphan featuring Sherlock Holmes and Moriarty.

Case of Witchcraft

A tale of witchcraft in the Northern Isles, in which some long-concealed secrets are revealed including about the Great Detective himself.

www.mxpublishing.com

Also From MX Publishing

The Affair In Transylvania

Holmes and Watson tackle Dracula in deepest Transylvania in this stunning adaptation by film director Gerry O'Hara

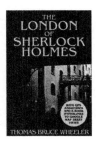

The London of Sherlock Holmes

400 locations including GPS co-ordinates that enable Google Street view of the locations around London in all the Homes stories

I Will Find The Answer

Sequel to Rendezvous At The Populaire, Holmes and Watson tackle Dr.Jekyll.

www.mxpublishing.com

Also From MX Publishing

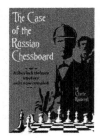

The Case of The Russian Chessboard

Short novel covering the dark world of Russian espionage sees Holmes and Watson on the world stage facing dark and complex enemies.

An Entirely New Country

Covers Arthur Conan Doyle's years at Undershaw where he wrote Hound of The Baskervilles. Foreword by Mark Gatiss (BBC's Sherlock).

Shadowblood

Sequel to Shadowfall, Holmes and Watson tackle blood magic, the vilest form of sorcery.

www.mxpublishing.com

Also From MX Publishing

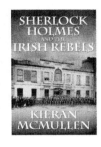

Sherlock Holmes and The Irish Rebels

It is early 1916 and the world is at war. Sherlock Holmes is well into his spy persona as Altamont.

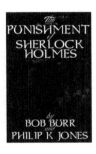

The Punishment of Sherlock Holmes

"deliberately and successfully funny"

The Sherlock Holmes Society of London

www.mxpublishing.com